DOUBLE-CROSSED!

Hoofs rattled like pebbles in a gourd. Yardigan whirled and fired toward a shadowy mounted figure and then dived for cover as he saw a rider raise a rifle. He rammed his skull against stone. His head seemed to explode. A rifle flamed and the slug whined off the rock beside him. He plunged his way into a thicket of cat-claw, thorns ripping at his face and head, his hands streaming with blood.

The full measure of what the riders were doing began to work insidiously into Yardigan's mind. They were destroying everything he owned, deliberately leaving him to rot in the desert sun.

"Bastards!" Yardigan mumbled venomously to himself. "Don't quit," a voice inside him said. Wes nodded. "I won't. They should have killed me. That was their big mistake...."

SOUTHWEST DRIFTER

GORDON D. SHIRREFFS

LEISURE BOOKS **NEW YORK CITY**

A LEISURE BOOK®

March 1997

Published by

Dorchester Publishing Co., Inc.
276 Fifth Avenue
New York, NY 10001

Printed in the United States of America.

ONE

The dry desert wind had shifted sometime after midnight and now swept down the canyon instead of across it. It moaned eerily as it swayed the dagger-tipped lechuguilla and rustled the stunted sotols. It hissed softly as it gathered up the fine, loose grit and gravel of the canyon bottom to sweep it down the canyon toward the wide, fan-shaped *bajada arenosa* that flowed down the slopes out onto the arid Lagarto Desierto, the great Desert of the Lizard, cursed by the sun and as waterless as the moon.

Wes Yardigan suddenly opened his eyes and raised his head to look toward the mouth of the mine tunnel. The thick darkness of the desert night had subtly altered to give way to the faintest of graying light. The dawn was not far off. Wes closed his eyes and rested his head on his crossed arms. Despite the padding of blankets beneath him he seemed to feel every minute bump, crack, and loose fragment of rock right through the bedding. He started to drift off into dreamless sleep, the sleep he so desperately needed. Something persisted in keeping him awake. He knew he could get no sleep as long as that prodding, irritating feeling was in his mind. It was a holdover from his days as an Army scout against the Apaches—something that had saved his life many a time. He opened his eyes. "Except once," he said. Wes shook his shaggy, dusty head. He had been alone in the brooding desert country too long. The weeks and weeks of solitude while he worked his claim had begun to work on his sensitive, imaginative mind.

"No, you weren't going to start talking out loud to yourself," said Wes. "You weren't going to get like the usual desert rat. Oh, no! Not ol' Wes Yardigan!" He closed his eyes again.

"Shut up," his mind discipline said curtly to him, "but don't go back to sleep."

This time he did not know how long he had been sleeping as he came bolt upright to instinctively drop a callused palm on the butt of his Colt. Wes stood up, taking care to keep his head bent to keep from smashing it against the low roof of the tunnel. He padded toward the mouth of the tunnel in his socked feet, a lath of a man attired only in his well-worn, long-handled johns, with the knees out and the drop seat flapping from the one button that still clung stubbornly to the worn fabric.

The wind moaned softly past the tunnel mouth. Wes flattened himself against the side of the tunnel and inched his way out onto the rough platform of rock he had cleared beyond the tunnel mouth. He went down on his knees and crawled to the low parapet he had constructed at the outer edge of the platform. Below it was a steep slope of mingled mine waste and detritus. He peered over the parapet. The canyon bottom was still thick in darkness. The wind died down, whimpering softly, then fading away down the canyon. It was getting close to dawn light. Wes could see the dull pewter sheen of the seep pool that formed in a shallow *tinaja,* or rock pan. The faint sound of a stifled bray came from up the canyon. Wes looked up that way. His good dun and his two burros grazed up there.

Wes rolled over the parapet to drop lightly onto the slope, bracing his legs as he half slid and half walked down the steep slope, with the soft hissing rush of the harsh rock and earth about his feet. There was a thicket of ocotillo at the bottom, and he went into a crouch as he reached it. The burro brayed again, sharply this time. A burro was as good as a watchdog, maybe better, at least when Indians were around.

Something moved in the darkness beyond the *tinaja.* The darkness blossomed a single orange-red flash, and the crisp sound of the report slammed back and forth between the canyon walls. Wes hit the ground, heedless of the knife-edged rock fragments, and fired twice toward where

6

he had seen the flash of the gun. A man yelled. Hoofs thudded on the hard ground. Wes leaped to his feet and plunged recklessly through a tangle of cat's-claw brush, cursing luridly as the thorns tore at his underwear and sank into his flesh. Another shot cracked out, and a slug keened within an inch of his head. Wes shook out two more rounds from the Colt.

Hoofs rattled like pebbles in a gourd. Wes whirled and fired toward a shadowy mounted figure and then dived for cover as he saw the rider raise a rifle. Wes rammed his skull against a rock. His head seemed to explode. A rifle flamed, and the slug whined off a rock beside Wes. He fought to keep his senses, but it was a losing battle. He began to crawl into the almost impenetrable tangle of shattered rock and thorny brush beyond the spring.

"Hola, Luis!" yelled a man from up the canyon. "Did you get him?"

"Yes, Vito! He is done for! Get Gonzalo!" yelled the mounted rifleman.

Wes pushed on, with the thorns ripping at his face and head. His hands were running with blood as he forced his way in deeper and deeper, hoping to God he would not rouse a sleeping diamondback. He could hear the raiders yelling back and forth behind him. Greasers! They were so damned sure of themselves. They must have crossed the Lagarto during the darkness of the night. Wes raised his head, and it seemed as though something split inside his skull. He seemed to hang on the very brink of a bottomless abyss and then he rolled over the edge and fell into it and he knew no more.

They had placed him on a vast gridiron and had stoked the fires beneath it while the sun beat upon his back to broil him thoroughly on both sides. Wes awoke to a world of excruciating pain. His brain thudded erratically against the inside of his skull casing. His eyes seemed to be on fire, and the thirst had penetrated into his very bone marrow. Wes slowly backed out of the thicket and crawled painfully across the harsh ground, the thorn-tipped brush tearing at him again. Every yard of the way was a yard cut from pure hell. He reached the *tinaja* and thrust his burning face into the water and as he did so he cautiously probed into his mat of reddish hair to feel for the wound. It was crusted with blood. He had done his best to brain himself.

He lay for a long time in the warm shade of the rock overhang, until the gathering heat of the morning threatened to completely enervate him. If he lay there much longer, he'd never be able to get up the slope to his tunnel. There was water and food up there, as well as protection from the burning sun that seemed to be concentrating its hellfire right down into Yardigan's Canyon to boil his brain inside his battered skull.

The burros and the horse would be gone. He fixed his wandering mind on the names he had heard during the fracas. "Luis, Vito, and Gonzalo," he said aloud. He touched his cracked lips with the tip of his tongue. "The Galeras Bunch," he added. He nodded his head. Luis and Vito were brothers, and Gonzalo Baca was their huge, dim-witted cousin. There were others of them as well. Bitterness added to the hate in his soul. They might just as well have made sure they had killed him if they had taken his horse and burros. The closest water was Papago Springs, about thirty miles away. Sometimes they dried up at this time of the year. Maybe he could make them on foot, but if the springs had run dry . . . He thrust the thought from his mind.

Wes cinched up his willpower and worked his way slowly across the bottom of the canyon and up the cruel, heat-shimmering slope with the sun pounding relentlessly against the back of his head and neck. His mouth gaped open against his will, and the lancing pain drove deeper and deeper into his brain, trying to get at the very root of his life. More than once the pain drove him sobbing to his knees as he climbed that hill of hell.

At last he rolled over the parapet and crawled like a wounded animal into the tunnel. Right away he knew they had been in there looking for his cache. His dirty blankets had been ripped into shreds. His good Chihuahua leather saddlebags had been slashed almost into thrums. The usual and rather pleasant astringent smell of the mine

8

tunnel was overhung by something foul. The acrid odor of urine and the thicker, cloying fecal odor indicated forcibly that the dirty scum had not been satisfied with ruining his possessions but had used his camping place as a latrine—with a whole gawd-damned desert and canyon to foul right outside of the tunnel. It was like their sort, thought Wes. They were more animal than men.

Wes walked back into the tunnel. Something cracked under his left foot. He bent down and picked it up, and looked through the cracked glass of the framed photograph into the young and smiling face of Lucy Fairbairn. "Maybe you were right after all," he said quietly. "Maybe I should have been satisfied with a good job."

He got his cached water olla. It had been untouched, more likely because they had not found it rather than for humane reasons. He scooped out a feebly swimming insect and placed it on the floor. "Go get your own water, you little bastard," he said sourly.

They had looted his war bag, taking his treasured tobacco as well as a quart bottle of Baconora brandy he had been saving to celebrate his first big strike. He did find a crumpled pack of Mex Lobo Negro cigarettes lying in the ashes of his fireplace. Further patient searching uncovered a partially used up block of lucifers. He lighted one of the strong, sweet-tasting cigarettes and looked about, taking stock. His Winchester '73 rifle and his good El Paso saddle were gone. They had taken all his food. He thought wryly of how long he had been yearning to hear another human voice and to see another human face in the past weeks. Well, he had had his wish. He only hoped one of his bullets had found its mark in one of those bastards.

"They got my dun," he said. "Damn them to hell!"

He got to his feet and walked to the mouth of the tunnel. If they hadn't known he had neatly taken himself out of the fight and was still alive, they likely would have made sure of him. He stepped out into the bright sunlight and felt the skin of his face tighten in the rays of the burning sun. He gingerly lifted one of the rocks of his parapet and thrust a hand down into the hole beneath it. His hand closed on his poke bag. He grinned, then winced as a lip cracked. "Bastards," he said in deep satisfaction. They had gotten just about everything but his life and the gold cache. "Dumb luck," he said.

He skipped back as the heat of the bare rock began to burn through his worn socks. He looked down the canyon and across the *bajada arenosa* to the Lagarto Desierto. It was a heat-shimmering hell on earth. Even a lizard would do well to live out there at this time of the year, and later . . . Wes drove that chilling thought from his mind. The heat waves rose from the bare surface of the baking ground, obscuring the vision and doing strange tricks to the eyesight. A lazy wind devil swept up from the ground surface to swirl voluptuously and then to sweep swiftly across the desert, disappearing as abruptly and as mysteriously as it had appeared. The full measure of Wes' predicament began to work insidiously in his mind, threatening to sap his manhood. "My cup runneth over," he said dryly.

"Don't quit," the mind voice said to him.

Wes nodded. "I won't. They should have killed me. It was their big mistake."

"The desert kills just as easily as the gun or the knife. Perhaps it does kill slower, but it is just as sure."

"I know. I know," said Wes patiently. He lighted another cigarette and looked down at the water pan. He could carry water in his two ollas. It would be best to travel at night, leaving as soon as the sun snagged itself on the heat-soaked mountains to the west. Beyond those mountains was the Colorado River. It was ten miles to the mountains and thirty miles beyond them to the river, but he'd have to cross the mountains in the dark. There might be water in the mountains. Tinajas Altas were up there and they usually had water all the year round. Usually . . . It would be green and gamey, but it would keep him alive long enough to reach the river. He could flag down a steamer once he reached the river, *if* he reached the Colorado.

"Jesus God," said Wes softly. Fear worked into his mind. He had no food. He'd have to leave while there was strength enough left in him to walk the thirty miles across the Lagarto at night to Papago Springs. Could a man walk thirty miles across that desert between sundown and sunup?

"You can't stay here," the mind voice said.

Wes laughed harshly. "I know! Crap or get off the pot!"

They had stolen his good boots. He'd have to wrap his feet in blanket strips. The dirty, thieving bastards! He closed his big, callused hands into rocky fists with the knuckles showing whitely through the taut, dirty skin. The payoff would be fists and boots if he could manage it. It was better that way.

"Stop feeling sorry for yourself," said the voice.

Wes turned his head as though the voice had come from the tunnel behind him. "For Christ's sake!" he snapped. He thrust forward his shaggy head. "I'm not sorry for myself! By God, I'm not! The pity will have to be for them, but none of it will come from me! Not from Wes Yardigan! You hear that?"

There was no answer. It seemed to Wes as though a soft and pleased chuckle came to him from deep within the tunnel.

Wes looked down into the canyon. "I've been out here alone too long!" he yelled.

"I've been out here alone too long," answered the canyon.

Wes grinned. "You, too?" he yelled.

"You, too? You, too? You, too?" answered the canyon.

Wes grinned again. "You damned well know it, canyon," he said in a low voice.

There was no hurry. He could not leave before sundown. He had enough water in the olla to last him through the worst heat of the day. He found another olla and fashioned crude caps and slings for both ollas. As he worked, the wind shifted and blew into the tunnel, stirring something that lay back in a partially dug drift. The smell of human waste came to Wes. He walked to the opening of the drift and looked down at the floor. Broken-backed books lay scattered about, and some leaves had been torn from them and befouled. He kicked one book out into better light. "Robert Burns," he said. He laughed. "The

11

best laid plans of mice and men. He knew what he was talking about." He lighted a cigarette. His little library was ruined. It was all he had had to remind him of his father. He picked up the books on his spade and dumped them into the fireplace. "You'll get decent burial," he said. "Cremation is more like it. Purifying fire." The hate for the Galeras Bunch was screwed a little tighter. "They leave nothing but ruin and waste," he said.

He awoke in the late afternoon. The air was deathly still. It lay in somnolent masses in the canyon and on the hills. The desert seemed to lie expectant. It was not yet time for the furnace winds to blow as they always did once the sun had died. He would have to buck those winds across the Lagarto in his flight to Papago Springs. "Flight," he said sarcastically. "Even a gawd-damned stupid buzzard can fly across the Lagarto Desierto, but a man can't. We ain't so damned smart after all."

Wes greased his feet and wrapped them in blanket strips. He fashioned a crude turban for his head and peered into the cracked mirror. "Like a gawd-damned Aaarab," he said. "More like one of the Three Wise Men. I sure could use one of their camels tonight."

He did not hear the voice anymore. There was no need for it to speak now. Wes knew what had to be done. He took out a very small part of his gold and folded it in a piece of leather, tied it together, and placed it inside his turban. The remainder he secreted under one of the flat stones in front of his fireplace, carefully sweeping ashes and dirt over it. He looked once more at the books, then snapped a match into life, touching it to the torn book leaves. He did not look back as he picked up his ollas and left the tunnel. Those books had been his friends and companions for the long weeks of solitude.

He filled his ollas and himself at the rock pan, wiping his mouth and beard as he stood up. "Lager beer," he said. "Oh, my God!"

He found his six-shooter in the brush. There was always that way out. Only a yellowbelly would take it, of course, but the Lagarto Desierto can make a yellowbelly out of the toughest of men. Wes opened the loading gate and turned the cylinder to count the cartridges. "One . . .

two . . . three . . . four . . . five . . ." His voice died away as he saw the empty sixth chamber. "Jesus God," he said in a strained voice. It had been his habit when working in the mine to load only five chambers, letting the hammer rest on the empty sixth to prevent accidental discharge if the handgun was dropped.

Wes stood there staring at the useless Colt. There were no cartridges in the tunnel. They had taken those as well as his rifle. "I could use the butt to pound coffee beans," he said. "That is, if I had me some coffee beans." He made as if to throw the useless weapon into the brush but thought better of it. It was a good gun, with a hand-honed action, and it had never failed him. He thrust it into the rope belt he had tied about his lean middle.

A fan of hot air moved across his sweating face. He looked back over his shoulder. The sun was just slipping behind the Tinajas Altas Mountains. It was the silent starting gun. Wes struck out for the mouth of the canyon. The darker area of the fan-shaped *bajada arenosa* sloped down toward the harsh desert floor. The idle thought ran through his mind that the *bajada arenosa* had been formed for ages past by the alluvial accumulation of silt and decomposed rock washed down the canyon in the time of the heavy spring rains. A lot of water. A veritable *river* of water. Thousands upon thousands of gallons of it had rushed out to a useless goal in the ever thirsty, sucking sands of the Lagarto Desierto. It was cruel, but then the whole damned country was cruel. Yet there was some gold and silver in the leached-out canyons. Maybe God had planned it that way. Hide the precious *oro* and *plata* in the wildest, most dangerous places for a man to search in during his insatiable hunger for riches. Let him *earn* it. The price was always high, one way or another.

Wes looked back at the silent, brooding canyon. "Damn you!" he yelled. "I *did* earn it!"

"Damn you," answered the canyon mechanically. "I *did* earn it!"

"What's the use?" said Wes. "It always has the last word."

The wind began to blow slowly and lethargically, as though it couldn't quite make up its lazy mind to blow at all. It would blow all right. It always did once the desert began to darken. Wes looked out across the Lagarto. A deep inner sickness welled up within him. The bravado vanished. This was no little drama to be played out before an admiring audience sharing a vicarious experience in the further adventures of Wes Yardigan. This was the real thing, a solo to be played out in private by Wes Yardigan himself.

He crossed the *bajada arenosa* feeling the stored-up heat strike up through his bandaged feet. The very thought of the darkened desert waiting out there for him like a quietly breathing beast of prey watching him, waiting first for his little mistakes, to play with him and toy with him until he made a bigger mistake, and then another until at last he made the final mistake, was enough to take all the spirit out of him even before he placed his feet on the true Lagarto.

Wes looked back at the darkened hills. "You and your damned gold," he said bitterly. "The least you could have done was to let a man have a decent strike instead of a stinking little poke of *chispas*. Just enough to lead him on, eh? Yeh, and all the time you were planning to let him run out his string. Is that all you've got to do?"

There wasn't any answer and there never would be an answer except for the rising moan of the night wind as it swept down from the heated hills to meet the cooling desert.

He struck the edge of the Lagarto at last. There were thickets of ocotillo, Mojave thorn, catclaw acacia and sotol palm. In the late spring the rains would pound down upon the hills and the desert, and the silty waters would flow down the canyons to form *bajada arenosas* such as the one he had just crossed. When the hot sun struck the once-flooded earth, there would be a sudden, almost miraculous outburst of splendid flowers. Blue lupine, varicolored mallows, desert goldpoppies, marigold, desert senna and zinnias. The cacti would blossom. The saguaro would put forth waxy white blooms. The cholla would flower. Wes spat dryly. "Don't send flowers to my funeral," he said. "Use the money for a more worthy cause. Like a damned good drunk for all the mourners."

It was still very hot on the Lagarto, and the thirst grew in him as he strode on into the darkness, but he would not drink. Not yet. He'd have to wait until it was almost unbearable.

One hour after he had left the canyon, a sling broke, and the olla struck the ground heavily and was shattered. He stood there foolishly, feeling the water soaking into his foot bandages. For some stupid reason he went down on his knees to pick up the fragments, and as he did so the second olla swung forward and struck the ground. Something cracked. Desperately he scooped up handfuls of the wet earth to plaster against the fat side of the olla, but it was no use. He snatched up the olla and tilted it to drain the water into his mouth with the mud dripping down into his beard. He felt the grit of the water between his teeth, and then it was all gone. He knelt there for a long time looking out into the windy darkness of the Lagarto. It was all part of the deadly game it played, like a cat toying with a wounded mouse or bird before it gave the final blessing of death.

"Go on back," the voice seemed to whisper in his ear.

"You bastard," said Wes. "Back there you told me I couldn't stay there."

There was a pause. "Yes," answered the voice. "And now you can't stay here."

"So I have to go back, eh?"

"That's about the size of it."

"What happens then?" asked Wes.

There wasn't any answer. There was no answer in the dry wind that swept across the deadly Lagarto Desierto. There is always an air of finality about the Lagarto Desierto.

Wes struck out, driving each leg stiffly forward, each step an effort of the will. His banged-up head ached intolerably, and thirst was brassy in his mouth and throat. "Yardigan's Canyon," he said. He laughed harshly. "More like Yardigan's Tomb!"

There was no comment from the mind voice. No answer in the voice of the night wind. Nothing from the Lagarto Desierto. There never would be an answer.

Once he turned and reached out a clawed and desperate

hand toward the distant and unseen Papago Springs. He walked on, praying aloud, for fear was a constant companion to him now. "I don't ask for much, Lord," he said in a low voice. "All I wanted was that little spread near the Chiricahuas. You know the one I mean. Good grazing. Plenty of water. Winter shelter. Streams full of trout and hills full of game. That was all I had in mind, Lord. But if this is the way it has to be, I'm not blaming anyone but a damned fool by the name of Wes Yardigan who had the infernal gall to think he could beat the Lagarto Desierto."

He looked over his shoulder as he wearily climbed the loose *bajada arenosa*. As he turned he caught the faintest of sparks out on the darkened desert. A moment later the spark flicked out again and then was gone. It wasn't a star. Too low for that. It wasn't a fire. Who'd build a fire on the Lagarto Desierto at night? It meant only one thing to Wes. Someone had lighted a cigarette out there, perhaps more than one of them. He dropped a hand to the butt of his useless Colt. The odds were that it was the Galeras pack coming back to the canyon. Maybe they had thought better of leaving without the gold.

Wes ran up the slope, throwing a glance over his shoulder now and then, but he did not see the sparks again. The desert was still dark in that thickest of darknesses before the rising of the new moon. He dropped belly-flat at the *tinaja* and drank his fill. He filled a rusted tin can with water and then slogged up the slope below his mine. There was no use in trying to hide in there. They could camp at the waterhole until thirst drove him into their hands. They'd wring the hiding place of the poke out of his hide.

Wes slanted across the slope to walk along a narrow and crumbling ledge that ran below a sheer rock face that had been left in ages past after the cracking of a great fault had sheared off thousands of tons of rock to tumble down the slope and clog the canyon below. Wes worked his way into the jumble of shattered rock and thorned brush. Some of the great boulders weighed many tons. If he had his rifle, he could hold them off indefinitely. If . . . The

16

heat had concentrated among the shattered rock, and the crawling itchiness of sweat broke out on his body.

The first faint promise of the rising new moon showed over the eastern mountains. There was nothing to do but wait for the Galeras Bunch and let them make their play. There was enough time to smoke his last cigarette. There wasn't much more that could happen to him now. Everything was going up the spout. The Lagarto Desierto had had its fun with Wes Yardigan. "Go on, damn you," he growled out into the darkness. "Get it over with!"

TWO

A hoof struck a rock at the mouth of the canyon and rang like a cracked bell. Voices murmured faintly. Minutes ticked past. Water splashed. They were watering their animals and themselves. Wes bellied out atop a large slab of rock that sent its stored-up heat right through his long johns into the skin of his belly. He could see two spots of light flaring up and dying away near the water hole. That accounted for two of them. The wind shifted a little, and he caught the blessed scent of tobacco smoke. Chihuahua! What a shot. Wes felt his palms itch for his Winchester .44/40.

The moonlight drifted leisurely down toward the depths of the canyon. One of the smokers stood up to look toward the mouth of Wes' mine. Wes could see the steeple-crowned hat and the dull sheen of coin-silver ornamentation. The second man stood up. He held a rifle in his hands. Wes lay flatter. Where the hell was the third man? The man with the rifle looked almost right at Wes. Any minute now!

"Hey, Wes! Hey, Wes! You up in that mine?" The voice echoed clearly up the canyon.

Wes stared down at the man who was calling to him. It was the familiar voice of Curly Killigrew. Surely he couldn't have been with the Galeras Bunch. Intense relief

17

flooded through Wes, and for a moment he almost thought he was going to wet his drawers.

"Hey, Wes! You up in your mine?" yelled Curly.

"Hey, Wes! You up in your mine? You up in your mine? You up in your mine?" echoed the canyon.

"Hey, Anselmo!" called Curly. "You think Wes has pulled foot?"

Anselmo? It was likely Anselmo Abeyta, as crooked as a dogleg fence. What was Curly doing with him? A cold and eerie feeling came over Wes. Maybe the two of them had been in on the raid. Anselmo had once ridden with the Galeras Bunch. He was their type. He'd put his grand-mother out to be a whore if there was a centavo of profit in it.

"Hey, Wes! Show yourself!" yelled Curly.

Wes took a chance and stood up, ready to drop in an instant. "What are you doing with him?" he yelled. "My camp just got jumped by Luis Galeras and his coyotes, and I'm not sure the two of you weren't in on the deal."

"You know me better'n that!" roared Curly angrily.

"Cleaned me out, the bastards," said Wes.

"I oughta punch in your head for sayin' something like that about ol' Curly Killigrew!"

"I still don't know what Anselmo Abeyta is doing with you," Wes challenged.

"Anselmo Abeyta?" said Curly. "He guided me here. Who else knew where you were?"

Who indeed, thought Wes. Anselmo Abeyta had known sure enough where Wes was working, for Wes had shied him out of there not more than two months past, fanning his rump with .44/40 rifle slugs.

"I come as the friend, Wes!" yelled Anselmo.

"Bullshit!" roared Wes. "I don't aim to come down there as long as you've got a gun or a knife handy, you garbage!"

Curly laughed. He slapped his thigh. "Same ol' Wes," he said in delight. "Go on, Anselmo. Beat it down the canyon and bring up the burro."

"Send him back to Papago Springs," said Wes.

"You dishonor me, Wes!" spluttered Anselmo. He crossed himself and held out his hands, palms upward.

"By the bones of my sainted mother! By the Sweet Names! By the very body of God! I come as the friend!"

"Bullshit!" roared Wes again.

"Bullshit!" echoed the canyon. This was great fun, a break in the deadly monotony of the Lagarto.

Curly walked across the canyon and placed his rifle on a flat rock. "You can get your hands on this first, Wes." He looked back at Anselmo. "Go get the burro! Pronto!" Anselmo got.

Curly looked up at Wes. "Likely you got so damned much gold you ain't interested in our humble food and Baconora brandy and some of them short six cigars you always was partial to, Wes."

Wes watched Anselmo walking down the canyon, the very picture of outraged virtue and honor. "What's your game, Curly?" he asked suspiciously. "I haven't bought *you* yet."

Curly unbuckled his gunbelt and dropped it to the ground. He walked to the waterhole and looked up at Wes. "My game is *gold,* Wes! All the gold you can get your dirty hands into." Curly grinned. That grin of his was famous all over Arizona. Curly could disarm a sidewinder with it. "Look, Wes! It was Buck Coulter sent me for you."

Wes stared at the man. He slid down the slope and picked up the rifle. Curly hunkered at the water hole, smoking a cigar and grinning at Wes like a damned Cheshire cat. "I knew that would bring you down," he said. He looked closely at Wes. "You sure you ain't a mite hill-nutty being out here too long alone?"

"I'm not hill-nutty enough to trust Anselmo Abeyta." Wes walked toward the water hole.

Curly wrinkled his nose. "You been short of water?" he asked.

"No," said Wes.

"Must be soap, then."

"Cut out the crap! What's this about Buck Coulter?"

Curly handed Wes a cigar and held a light for it. "He hasn't got a warrant for you, if that's what's worrying you," said Curly. "You done something you shouldn't have?"

19

"Not in Eden City," said Wes. "I'm not vouching for the rest of the Territory."

Curly inspected his cigar. "Lots of people wondering why you stay out here on the Lagarto, so close to the border, too."

"You're a damned liar," said Wes.

Curly shrugged. "I seen Lucy Fairbairn some time back."

Wes took the cigar from his mouth. "She mention me?"

Curly spat to one side. "Why should she, amigo?"

Wes took a deep breath. "She isn't married or anything like that, is she?"

Curly shook his head. "You still got a soft spot in your skull for her, ain't you?"

Wes replaced the cigar in his mouth. "How's Buck's leg?"

"It ain't any better," said Curly.

"I might have known," said Wes quietly.

"Look, Wes! You got to stop blamin' yourself for that leg of his. You wasn't the one that shot him, you know."

"No," said Wes slowly, "but he didn't have to risk his life by coming back to save mine. He was in the clear. No one would have blamed him for keeping on going. Least of all *me*!"

"That wasn't Buck Coulter's way, Wes, and you know it! He wasn't going to let any Apache buck gut you like a rabbit while you was lying there helpless. Don't worry about Buck. He does right well for himself in Eden City." Curly rubbed his jaw and looked sideways at Wes. "Yeh, he sure does," he added in an odd voice.

"Can he ride like he used to?" demanded Wes. "Can he cover twenty miles on foot between sundown and sunup?"

"Look, Wes," said Curly patiently, as though he were talking to a small child. "Buck was gettin' on in years even when he saved your life and stopped an Apache bullet with his left leg. He's doing all right in Eden City, like I said. Owns a piece of Duke Draegar's Buckhorn, as well as being Chief Marshal of Eden City. Got his hands

20

in other things, too. Forget about his leg, Wes. Buck Coulter is a legend in his time. He still thinks a lot of you, likely more than anyone else he knows." Curly relighted his cigar and looked curiously at Wes. "For God's sake," he added quietly. "That ain't why you shy away from Eden City and stay out here on the Lagarto all by yourself, is it?"

Wes shook his head. "No." He looked up at the moonlit sky. "Maybe I like the Lagarto, as deadly as it is. There's a cleanness about it. It's hard to explain."

"I'll bet," said Curly softly. He reached behind a rock and withdrew a bottle. He pulled the cork out with his teeth and handed the bottle to Wes. "Here," he said. "You'll need some of this before I tell you why me and Anselmo come for you."

Wes upended the bottle and drank deeply. He lowered it and sighed in satisfaction. "I needed that," he said. He looked sideways at Curly. "Shoot," he added. He raised the bottle to his lips and started to drink.

"The Lost Killdevil," said Curly.

Wes sprayed out the good brandy before he could help it. He wiped his mouth and beard and looked incredulously at Curly. "You're pulling my leg," he said.

Curly shook his head. "You heard me," he said.

Wes upended the bottle and drank deeply. He could feel the good brandy working in his gut. He placed the bottle on a rock. "You could have saved yourself a hard ride out here and your brandy as well," he said. "The Lost Killdevil is a myth, a legend, a Mexican fairytale told by the drunks in every cantina in Eden City's Chile Town. Every time you hear that tale, it gets better and better."

"I got to admit that the story had been colored up and embroidered all to hell, Wes," Curly said. "Likely ol' Jesus Melgosa wouldn't recognize it hisself."

"Jesus Melgosa was a damned old liar," said Wes. "He never got his gold out of the Espantosa Mountains."

Curly eyed his cigar. "But he *did* have gold," he said quietly.

"Thirty years ago! Before the Civil War!"

Curly looked sideways at Wes with half-closed eyes.

"Don't you con me, Wes," he said softly. "You know as well as I do that Jesus Melgosa did get his gold out of the Espantosa. And, what is more, he left a helluva lot more gold in them damned mountains than he ever took out of them!"

Wes laughed. "Man, you *are* sick! The mine is a myth. That's how it got its name. It would kill the devil if he tried to find it."

Curly looked back over his shoulder as though someone were listening. "Or maybe someone would kill the devil if he did find it." He looked back at Wes. "If Buck Coulter himself was to tell you we got a good lead on the Lost Killdevil, would you believe it?"

Wes relighted his cigar. He looked at Curly speculatively. "Well," he said thoughtfully.

Curly saw the slight beginnings of an opening. "He's got it, Wes! He thinks so much of it that he's formed a partnership with me and Anselmo to go look for the Lost Killdevil."

"Anselmo Abeyta," said Wes. He spat to one side.

"He knows the Espantosas better than any living man," said Curly shrewdly.

Wes leaned forward. His pride had been stung, as Curly had anticipated. Wes stabbed a hard forefinger down on Curly's thigh. "No man living knows those mountains better than I do," he said hotly.

"That is perhaps so," said the soft voice just behind Wes.

Wes moved like a cat. He was on his feet, swinging the rifle to cover Anselmo's shrinking gut, levering a round into the chamber in fluid action. The muzzle came to rest two inches from a spot just above Anselmo's big gun-belt buckle.

Anselmo smiled uneasily. "Put down that rifle, Wes. I could have killed you easily with the knife or the gun in the past few minutes, and you never would have known what hit you."

Wes studied the dark face of the Mexican. Anselmo might have been fairly presentable in his youth, say about the time he learned to toddle, but a hard life along the border, devoted to crime and tequila, in the order named,

22

had made a lifetime mark on his face. One hard brown eye was fixed on Wes, but the other eye had a will and a way of its own. That eye seemed to wander a little, giving a person the uneasy feeling as to *which* eye was really on him. Wes had the hunch that more than a few men might have died figuring that out while Anselmo himself was busy with knife or gun.

"Anselmo ain't about to cross Buck Coulter, Wes," said Curly. "He knows what would happen to him if he crossed you."

Wes spat to one side. "I buy nothing good about him," he said coldly.

Anselmo deftly crossed himself. "By the bones of my sainted grandmother," he said. "You can trust me now, Wes."

"You likely dug up her sainted bones and strung them together with wire to sell to some medical college," said Wes. "Anything to make a peso, eh, Anselmo?"

Both eyes now fixed themselves on Wes in a basilisk stare; then the wandering eye could no longer hold it and it moved off on its own, letting the fixed eye handle the situation alone. "Ha, ha," said Anselmo between his teeth. "You are always the great joker, Wes."

"Ha, ha," mimicked Wes.

"Grub pile, Anselmo," said Curly. "We've got to get some strength into Wes for the ride back to Eden City."

"I'm not going anywhere," said Wes.

Curly gathered together some dry wood and began to shave off splinters to start a fire. "They say ol' Luke Fairbairn has got a lead on the Lost Killdevil, too," he said casually.

Wes upended the bottle. He lowered it. "That old fool has had a lead on the Lost Killdevil for thirty years," he said sourly.

Curly shrugged. He lighted the shavings and hunkered back on his heels. "This time he's supposed to have the goods," he said.

"I thought Buck Coulter had the goods," said Wes.

Curly nodded. "It's a long story," he said. He fed the fire. "Lucy is all the old man has left now since Lucy's pa was killed in the Espantosas."

23

Wes narrowed his eyes. "Jim Fairbairn dead?" He shook his head. "I never thought he was loco enough to go after Killdevil."

Curly looked sideways at Wes. "Likely he wasn't, leastways in times past, but, like I said, this time the old man has a lead that's pretty good. Some say that's why Jim was killed."

"Killed?" said Wes. "Who did it?"

"Murder," said Anselmo as he led up a laden burro. "Just another one to add to the list of unsolved murders in the bloody Espantosas."

"Cut that crap," said Curly. "It's likely the Apaches."

Anselmo shook his head. "Jim was killed near Ojo del Muerto, the Eye of Death, beneath Cuchillo Peak. Do the Apaches go near that place of death? No!"

"He's got something there," said Wes.

Curly placed the battered spider over the flames and took a chunk of bacon from Anselmo's hand. "It's Lucy who goes with the old man now."

Wes stared at him. "Into the Espantosas?"

"Where else?" said Anselmo. He shrugged. "If one looks for the Killdevil, one must look in the Espantosas. *No es verdad?*"

Wes nodded. "I'll buy that," he agreed. "But to take a girl like Lucy into them on a hunt for a mine that maybe doesn't even exist . . ." He shook his head.

"She ain't no girl now," said Curly. He looked at Anselmo. "How about that?"

Anselmo's two eyes coordinated long enough to roll upward. "That is so!" he said with ecstasy in his voice.

Wes stirred a little. "Cut it," he said. "You aren't leading me up the garden path. We were talking about a lost mine, not about Lucy Fairbairn."

"So we was," said Curly. He sliced the bacon. "The four of us can make a killin', Wes."

"Four?" said Wes. He sniffed the good smoked bacon.

Anselmo had filled the smoke stained coffee pot. He placed it in the embers to one side of the fire. "Buck, Curly, you, and me, Wes," he said. He grinned.

24

"Why?" said Wes. "Why such a curious combination?"

Curly began to slice a loaf of bread. "Buck has the lead. Anselmo knows more about minerals and suchlike than any of us do, even you, Wes. Me, I know the Espantosas fairly well, and Buck trusts me. We need you, Wes. Buck can't get around like we can. We got good legs, eh, Wes?"

Wes looked down at Curly's bowed legs. "I've seen prettier legs on Prescott Street in Eden City when the whores take the sun on a windy day," he said. He rubbed his jaw. "What I don't get through my cabeza is this: if Buck is doing as well as you say he is, why does he want to go foolin' around after the Lost Killdevil?"

"Well," said Curly. "Buck don't want to spend the rest of his life sitting in the stool pigeon's post in the Buckhorn and chousin' drunks off Front Street. Sure, he's got *some* money, but no one knows how much."

"Where'd he get it?" asked Wes quietly.

"Gambling," said Anselmo.

"That doesn't figure," said Wes. "I'm better at gambling than he is and I never won any decent pots."

"He's got a piece of the Buckhorn," said Curly.

"I don't get that," said Wes. "He and Duke Dracgar were always like oil and water. They just don't mix."

Anselmo placed a crock of beans into the ashes. "They say he set Sophie Belaire up in her new parlor house on Prescott Street."

Wes laughed. "That's the best yet! Anytime Sophie Belaire had to have help on a business deal."

"Well, it's so," insisted Curly. "You know how Sophie feels toward Buck."

Wes nodded. He plucked the makings from Curly's shirt pocket and shaped a cigarette. An odd, crawling feeling of distaste had come over him. He was thinking of Buck Coulter—*the* Buck Coulter—making a living by playing stool pigeon for a tinhorn like Duke Draegar and maybe pimping for Sophie Belaire. Buck Coulter, a legend in his time ... Maybe the country should pension off young heroes when their blood is hot and their feet are not of clay. Most of them did not seem capable of keeping

25

up the reputations that had been blown out of all semblance to reality in the minds of the hero-worshipping and fickle public.

"Buck is ambitious," said Curly. He removed the spider from the fire and drained off the grease. "He needs money to float a few big investment ideas of his."

Wes nodded. "Buck has a great buiness head," he said dryly. "I remember a few business ventures of his some years past. I'd almost bet he's still in hock for some of them."

Curly did not look at him. "He's learned a lot since then, Wes," he said. He stirred the beans. "We can't lose on this deal, Wes."

"What's this lead you have?" said Wes. He was getting bored with the whole procedure, but it wasn't polite to tell them so until after he had eaten their food.

Neither Anselmo nor Curly spoke as Curly ladled out the food into tin plates. Wes studied their faces in the firelight. They were holding something back from him, something they seemed quite sure would sell him on a hunt for the Lost Killdevil in the mountains of the damned, the bloody Espantosas. Wes never wanted to go into those mountains again. Too much of his early history had been entangled with the Espantosas. Maybe that was why he preferred such lonely, forgotten places as the Lagarto Desierto.

Curly finished eating and swabbed out his plate with a chunk of bread. "Jesus Melgosa left a *derrotero*," he said.

"Jesus God!" said Wes. He rolled his eyes upward. "Spare me this, O Lord! I've suffered enough this last twenty-four hours. I'm not complaining, you understand, but don't punish me with Jesus Melgosa and his *derrotero!*" He looked at Curly. "Are you soft in the cabeza like the yellow of an egg? Jesus Melgosa left the *derrotero!* Oh, my God! I've heard everything now! Every drunken Mexican in Chile Town can supply you with the only *authentic derrotero* of Jesus Melgosa's Lost Killdevil—left to him by his sainted grandfather, you understand? But to you, my friend, I will sell that precious *derrotero* for the price of a few drinks. I do not want to be rich, señor. Only

26

to be happy is all I wish. I have taken a vow never to be rich, therefore I must remain poor until the end of my days." Wes spat into the fire and raised his coffee cup. "My God! The next day he's nursing a helluva tequila hangover while he scrapes an old javelina hide to get ready to make the only *authentic derrotero* of Jesus Melgosa to sell to the next sucker."

"Listen to him," said Curly in disgust.

Anselmo nodded. "The stage lost a great performer when Wes Yardigan decided to become a wealthy prospector."

"Can't you believe there might just be a real *derrotero* left by Jesus Melgosa?" demanded Curly.

Wes jerked a thumb up toward his mine. "That's *my* Lost Killdevil, and I didn't need any damned *derrotero* to find it!"

"Show him, Anselmo," said Curly quietly.

Anselmo reached inside his jacket and withdrew a fold of hide. Carefully he unrolled it and placed it on the flat rock in front of Wes. He sat back on his heels and watched Wes.

The piece of parchment-thin hide was roughly triangular in shape, with two raw-looking edges, as though it had recently been torn from a larger piece or perhaps two pieces of about equal size. The third edge was wrinkled and cracked with age. Wes leaned forward and studied it. He had seen many of these *derroteros*, or charts. Some of them had simply been sets of directions, or waybills, while others were truly charts. Some had been very old, some new, and others had been artificially aged. This hide *was* old, there was no doubt in Wes' mind about that. There were certain things on such a chart that would be obvious if one was to search for the Lost Killdevil. Wes noticed something strange, but his face did not change expression. He was too good a poker player for that. He was acutely conscious of the eyes of his two companions being fixed on his face for the slightest indication of what he felt. Something caught his eye, but he quickly passed over it. He had been fooled before. Still . . .

"Well," said Curly.

"It's old," said Wes. He began to roll a cigarette. "If it

is authentic, as you claim it to be, you won't get very far with this one piece of it."

"We never said we would," said Curly.

"The *derrotero* is in three pieces," said Anselmo. "The Señor Buck has the piece that belongs here." He placed a finger on the lower part of the hide. "He let us take this piece along to convince you, Wes."

"He'd never have seen you again if you had both pieces in your hands," said Wes dryly. He looked at Curly. "Who's got the other piece?"

Curly shrugged. "Quién sabe?" he said. He did not sound very convincing. "Buck thinks we've got enough of the *derrotero* to make a damned good try for it."

Wes lighted the cigarette. "How did you sterling characters happen to get hold of the two pieces you have?" he murmured.

Anselmo and Curly had played much poker in their time, too. Their faces were masks as they looked at Wes. Curly grinned. "What difference does that make, Wes?" he asked. "We've got 'em, ain't we? That should be enough for you, eh? That is why we came for you to offer you a quarter share."

Wes shook his head. "There was only one man who could read such a *derrotero*," he lied. "Eusebio Ochoa, the man who raised me as his own son when I lost my family. Eusebio Ochoa is dead. The dead do not talk."

"Murdered in the Espantosas," said Curly. He refilled the coffee cups. He looked sideways at Wes.

"Eusebio Ochoa is dead," admitted Anselmo, "but his memory did not die with him. That memory lives on in you, Wes. No other man had the lore of lost mines and of the Espantosas so well as him. No other man hunted as persistently for the Lost Killdevil as he did. He died in that search after you had left those mountains. Some say he would still be alive if you had not left him, Wes."

"God strike you dead for such a lie!" said Wes.

"It is not *I* who says such things," said Anselmo. "May this canyon crumble about us if that is not the truth!"

A rock fell from the sheer wall above Wes' mine and shattered on the slope far below. Anselmo's eyes widened in disbelief. He crossed himself. Another rock broke loose and fell after the first one.

"This happen often?" Curly asked nervously.

"Usually at night," said Wes. "Rocks cool and break off. Takes a while to get used to it. Might be just a rockfall and then again it might not. Sometimes you get the feeling you're being watched by someone or something up there, but you never see anything."

"Like the Espantosas," said Anselmo soberly.

Wes glanced quickly at the Mexican. Anselmo had the uncanny ability to read or guess what was in Wes' mind when he spoke about the Espantosas. The name itself meant 'haunted' or 'horrible,' named with that apt description the Spaniards have for such things. Some said that man had given them their eerie reputation, while others, particularly the Apaches, Papagos, and Pimas, claimed that it was of supernatural origin. There were certain areas in those mountains that the Apaches shunned, and a Papago or a Pima would not even enter the foothills in broad daylight.

"We can pull out of here yet tonight," said Curly.

"Leave me some cartridges, one of your rifles, and that burrito," said Wes. "I'll pay you out of my poke."

"You ain't using your cabeza, Wes," said Curly angrily.

"I know what I've got here," said Wes firmly. "I don't know what you'll get, besides your death, in those damned Espantosas." He placed his hand on Curly's rifle.

Another rock fell, and then another and yet another. Echo chased after echo down the canyon.

"Do I get what I want?" said Wes. He raised the rifle.

"Supposin' we don't agree?" said Curly truculently.

The rifle muzzle swung back and forth in an arc. "I've already got the rifle," Wes said pointedly.

A large slab of rock broke loose and shattered on the slope, casting rock fragments toward the three men. They ran down the canyon. There was a splintering of rock followed by a splitting, cracking sound like river ice breaking in the spring sun. Tons and tons of rock fell into the canyon while a great veil of bitter dust rose above it.

Anselmo and Curly ran back to get the horses and the burro, snatching up whatever gear they could. Wes looked up. "Run, you bastards! Run!" The whole face of the cliff was leaning outward. Thousands of tons of rock and earth broke loose with a reverberating roar that filled the canyon and thundered far out onto the dreaming Lagarto Desierto. Thick, billowing clouds of acrid dust filled the canyon. The very ground shook beneath their feet.

The mine entrance vanished beneath tons of rock, and great boulders smashed down on the *tinaja* and seep, concealing it forever. The echoes died away, and the wind drifted the dust out toward the Lagarto, dimming the moonlight.

Wes reached into one of the zurróns on the burro's back and pulled out a fresh bottle of Baconora. He drank deeply and wiped his mouth. "All gone," he said quietly. "Mine, poke, water, horse, burritos, clothing, food, and rifle. Naked came I into this world of woe and naked will I leave it."

Without a word Curly and Anselmo mounted their horses. Wes placed a long leg over the neck of the patient, dusty burro and eased his lean rump between the tops of the zurróns. They all rode down the canyon without a backward glance. Wes' turban sagged forward to lean rakishly over one eye. He was slightly drunk and getting drunker by the minute. Neither of the other two would look back and smile at him and his lugubrious appearance. That, they did not dare to do.

THREE

The Espantosa Mountains stood up starkly from the more level land that lay to the south and west of the range, trending down into the bottomlands of the San Augustin River. In the old days the towering range had been a landmark for the Spanish conquistadores and padres who had come up from Sonora in their ceaseless quest for gold and converts. In those days the mountains had been named by the Spaniards as the Sierra de Espuma, or Foam Mountain, because of the outstanding white streak of rock that ran just under the rim of the western escarpment. The local Indians had always believed that the streak marked the height of a great flood that had covered the land beyond the memory of man. It had been the Mexicans who had changed the name of the Sierra de Espuma to the Sierra Espantosa, or Frightful Mountain; the Espantosas had well earned that name.

Wes Yardigan looked often and long at the Espantosas as he and his two companions rode steadily west along the base of the foothills on their way to the fleshpots of Eden City, marked against the gathering dusk by twinkling yellow lights and a scarf of smoke that stained the sunset. Wes knew the Espantosas well. God, how he knew them! The towering natural ramparts that thrust themselves in tin-cut silhouette against the darkening sky seemed like the ramparts of some medieval fortress, thrown up in eons past by violent volcanic upheavals, then riven and carved into fantastic shapes by the uneasy movements of the cooling earth and later eroded by the constant downpourings of the succeeding pluvial ages. Beyond the ramparts, in the inner keep of the Espantosas, was a phantasm of hundreds of square miles of draws, arroyos, and canyons, crossing and crisscrossing, interlocking in a hopeless maze of peaks and shattered masses of basaltic and granitic rock. Matting the higher elevations were dense thickets of scrub oak, mesquite, and juniper, while far below in the canyons and the dry stream beds were almost impenetrable abatis of shattered knife-edged rock and fallen timbers, interlaced with chevaux-de-frise of catclaw and jumping cholla, crucifixion thorn, and wait-a-bit brush. These lower areas were infested with sidewinders and thick-bodied diamondbacks, as well as the small, secretive, and deadly Sonoran coral snake.

Wes knew the Espantosas, perhaps better than any living man, as Curly had hinted. He had been born in a lower canyon beneath the looming mountains. The ranch house that had been his home since his birth until he was five years old now lay a blackened ruin in an atmosphere of unutterable loneliness. All of Wes' natural family lay buried in that canyon in mounded graves now overgrown with thorny brush. His father and his mother, an older sister, and an infant brother whom he could barely remember. Chiricahuas and Tontos had managed at last to surprise the tough Pennsylvanian who had made his home in the Espantosas at the close of the Civil War. The vaqueros had been cut off and slaughtered in the canyons. Wes himself, in later years, had buried such parts of some of their skeletons as had remained after the animals had finished with them. He himself had managed to hide in among the shattered rock slabs of a slope above the canyon. If he had made one outcry, those bushy-headed devils would have found him. He had not made an outcry, nor had he made any sound when old Eusebio Ochoa, his father's good friend, had found him two days later, a strangely silent boy with great, staring eyes whom Eusebio had taken to his jacal and raised as his own son.

Wes fashioned a cigarette, half listening to the idle chatter of Curly and Anselmo. They weren't talking about the Lost Killdevil now. There were other interests in Eden City. Wes lighted the cigarette. No man had known the Espantosas better than Eusebio Ochoa. Some said he had been the only friend of the legendary Jesus Melgosa, that strange and bloody man who had started the tale of the Lost Killdevil, whether it was real or imaginary. No one really knew, but Eusebio Ochoa had devoted his later life in searching for the lost mine. It had paid him off in the usual coin. Sudden death in a lonely canyon, and no one to know the killer.

Wes looked back over his shoulder at the great, naked finger of rock that towered up from within the inner keep of the Espantosas. Sangre Cuchillo Peak. It had once been simply Cuchillo Peak, or Knife Peak. The Sangre had been added in later years. Sangre, or Bloody Knife Peak. The Spaniards and the Mexicans always had a fascination for blood. Again, the peak had earned the adjective. At its base, half hidden in a great rock vault carved into the side of the peak and overgrown with trees and brush, was Ojo del Muerto Springs—The Eye of Death. This time the

Spaniards had merely adopted the Apache name for the place. No one knew why it had originally been so named. It, too, had later earned its name. Few men died natural deaths in the Espantosas.

"For God's sake, Wes!" Curly said suddenly. "Stop lookin' at them gawd-damned mountains! That look on your face is enough to put the chills into a man!"

Wes tore his eyes from the Espantosas. Curly had partially staked him to a new outfit and a horse in Medano. Wes had been talkative enough until he had caught his first sight of the Espantosas, still miles away. After that he had become silent, and the others, sensing his feeling, had left him alone.

Anselmo deftly shaped a cigarette and thrust it into his mouth. He glanced sideways at Wes as he lighted the quirley. "It is said that one must always come back to them, is that not so, Wes?" he asked.

Wes glanced at him. It was not a joke. Anselmo knew the old local superstition well enough and, what is more, he believed in it.

"What is up there, eh, Señor Wes?" the Mexican asked softly. "Much gold? Perhaps the wealth of a Montezuma?"

"You're doing the talking," Wes said dryly.

The one fixed eye tried to probe into Wes' eyes. "Is it perhaps that the brave Señor Yardigan, the much of a man, might be afraid of those mountains?"

Curly grinned. "What's he got to be afraid of up there?"

"The things *we* are afraid of, amigo. The men who have been murdered in the lonely canyons. The men who have entered there and have never been seen again. The headless bodies that have been found. The nameless something that guards the Lost Killdevil." Anselmo looked at Wes. "This, Wes knows well, for was he not born in the shadows of the Espantosas?"

"That ain't true, is it, Wes?" asked Curly.

Wes felt for the makings. "That much is true," he admitted.

"I knew you lived around them for years. Never knew you was *born* in 'em."

33

Wes began to shape a cigarette. "You never asked me," he said quietly.

"Is what he says true?" Curly asked. "About the fear, I mean?"

Wes snapped the match into a quick spurt of bright yellow and applied it to the twisted tip of the cigarette. For those few seconds Curly saw the look in Wes' eyes and he had the answer to his question.

A Standard freight locomotive hauling a string of ore cars whistled stridently for the crossing near the bridge over the dry San Augustin. Eden City had grown greatly in size since the last time Wes had seen it. Before the Civil War it had been a wide place in the road called Quatro Jacales. Northerners had named it Unionville in the spring of 1861. When all Federal troops had left Arizona in 1862, the Texas Mounted Rifles had renamed the place Secessionville. Shortly after the Texans had retreated to New Mexico, a mixed band of Chiricahuas, Mimbrenos, and Tontos had wiped out Secessionville's little population and had burned the place to the ground. Someone with a clumsy sense of humor had named it Eden after the war for the simple reason that it was anything *but* an Eden. The railroad had started creeping west to the Colorado River, reached and passed Eden, leaving a legacy of boom times. Civic pride had added City to the name. Eden City wasn't a city yet, but it was damned well putting its navel down into the hot sand trying to be one.

"Lager beer," said Wes suddenly.

Curly guffawed. "Now, how the hell did you know what I was just thinkin' about?"

"What else is there to think about right now?" asked Wes.

"There is salt in that which you say, amigo" said Anselmo wisely.

"Salt sure goes good in lager beer," responded Curly. "Hawww!"

"You've been around burros too long," said Wes.

"What's first on the agenda, as they say?" said Curly.

34

Wes wet his dry lips. "That's second, Curly," he said.

Curly grinned. "Wrong this time, amigo. We need a drink or two to cut the dust. You can see Buck. The girls can wait for their fun."

"Listen to him!" said Anselmo. "Such modesty!"

Front Street was booming as the three dusty riders slanted through the traffic toward the Buckhorn Saloon, gracing the northeast corner of Front and Prescott, the two main right-angled streets of Eden City.

Curly swung down from his horse and slapped the dust from his clothing. He looked at the thronging men—ranchers and cowpokes, miners and men from the stamping mills in the nearby San Augustin Hills. "At least one of them will be dead before midnight," he said soberly.

"How so?" asked Wes, curious.

"Eden City has had a man for dinner just about every Saturday night for the past two years," said Curly.

"Sometimes more," added Anselmo. "Three months ago four men died between sundown and sunup."

"In one fracas?" Wes asked. He whistled softly.

"Four separate fights," said the Mexican.

"You didn't count that stabbing down in Chile Town, amigo," Curly said to Anselmo.

Anselmo shrugged. "You Yanquis do not count the killing of us greasers," he said coldly.

"You know I don't feel like that," Curly protested.

Anselmo glanced at Wes. "No, not you," he said. His unspoken meaning was plain enough.

"Go scratch your ass, Anselmo," said Wes.

"By God," said Curly. "I'll have to keep each of you at opposite ends of the bar and stay myself in the middle to maintain the peace, as they say!"

"With the free lunch at one end?" said Wes. "Fat chance."

Even Anselmo had to smile at that one. Curly's depredations on the magnificent free lunches of Eden City were almost a local tradition.

Wes pushed through the batwings of the Buckhorn and blinked his eyes in astonishment. "Chihuahua!" he said.

"I told you it was really something," said Curly.

"If Buck has a piece of this, he's doing all right," said

Wes. When Wes had frequented the Buckhorn in years past, it had been one store, rather long and narrow, but now the walls of the two adjoining stores had been knocked out to make a large establishment crammed with gambling tables and booths and tables for serious drinking. Crystal chandeliers hung from the ceiling. Their brilliant light reflected from the rows and rows of bottles and the full-length mirrors behind them. The long mahogany bar was crowded with men, and the gambling tables were doing a booming business.

Wes looked down at his dusty trail clothing and scarred boots. "You sure we're welcome here, Curly?" he asked.

Curly grinned. "You could come in here mother naked as long as you was concealing your privates with a filled wallet, Wes."

Wes looked over the heads of the crowd toward the tall stool that stood upon a box against the rear wall of the establishment. A man was doing 'stool-pigeon' duty in it. Even at that distance Wes recognized the man. He worked his way through the crowd, keeping his eyes on Buck Coulter.

Buck wore his fine Stetson slanted on the back of his dark hair, now well toned with gray at the sides. His mustache was also graying. A long cigar was stuck in the side of his mouth, and a faint wraith of tobacco smoke drifted about his lean face, but the light gray eyes were alert, scanning the crowd, missing nothing. Those eyes instinctively flicked toward Wes, and Buck took the cigar from his mouth. A pleased smile came over his face.

"Buck!" said Wes. "Buck Coulter!"

Buck thrust out a hand. "Well, I'll be go to hell," he said. "They *did* get you out of those damned hills, eh, boy? You're a sight uglier than usual, but all the same it's fine to see you!"

Wes grinned self-consciously. Men glanced at him. To be recognized as a friend by Buck Coulter—*the* Buck Coulter—was the accolade of honor in Arizona Territory.

Wes flicked a glance at the heavy, silver-topped ebony cane that stood beside the stool. Buck had used a cane for about a year after the Apache bullet had chewed into the

36

thighbone, and later only in damp weather, when the wound bothered him.

"Carry it all the time now, boy," said Buck cheerfully. "Classy bit of goods, eh?" He relighted his cigar. "Bone splinters work out now and then. Once they're all out, I'll be as good as new." There was conviction lacking in his tone. A sort of fatalistic bravado that didn't quite come off.

Wes looked out over the crowd. "How do you keep track of all of them?" he asked.

Buck shrugged. "You get to know them all, Wes. The tinhorns, cheats, pickpockets, grifters, con men, and troublesome drunks. Once in a while you get a different one. The one who comes in quietly, does his drinking, and then makes his play, whatever it is." The clear gray eyes settled on Wes. "A man such as you, Wes. Hard to tell what a man like you is thinking."

"Is it that obvious?" said Wes. He was puzzled and a little uneasy. He had never quite thought of himself in that sort of light.

"You haven't changed much," said Buck.

Their eyes met, and Wes looked away. There was something behind Buck's voice, pleasant as it was. It might be the same buried thought that was in Wes' mind, the thought that refused to stay in its grave. Wes didn't really know, but there had been times when he had thought Buck resented his crippling wound and the cause for which he had suffered it. A man like Buck Coulter, a living legend in his time, needed all his faculties in a land where physical prowess and deadly skill were needed to survive. Such a man could only resent living out his later life as a cripple, perhaps as an object of pity to others. A man like Buck Coulter could never stand for that.

"I'll be off duty in an hour," said Buck. He smiled. "Have to keep the rules, even if I am one of the partners here, Wes. That's part of the deal, boy."

"With Duke Draegar," said Wes dryly.

Buck's eyes narrowed. "I know how you feel about him," he said, "but you don't work with him, Wes."

"It doesn't matter to me, Buck," said Wes. "I don't work for him, like you said."

Buck seemed a little annoyed. "Get this straight," he said. "I work *with* him, not *for* him." He looked over Wes' head. "Your two partners are drinking. How are you fixed for dinero, Wes?"

"Curly has been backing me," Wes said.

Buck eased himself down from the stool and gripped the cane. "Wait a minute," he said. "There's Duke. I'll get some ready money for you, boy. I want to see you alone at my quarters in the Territorial House. Say ten o'clock? Keno?"

Wes nodded. Duke Draegar stood just outside the half-open door to his office. He was watching the crowd, but there was no expression on his smooth, rounded face. Likely adding up the estimated take for the night, the cold-gutted shark, thought Wes. Draegar turned slightly toward Buck as Buck spoke to him, but his half-veiled eyes glanced at Wes first and then back at the crowd. He seemed to be annoyed.

Wes took a few steps toward them and then stopped as he heard Duke's testy reply to a question Buck had asked him. "You're into me too damned heavy as it is, Buck. I'm not sure I want to advance you any more."

"You know I'm good for it, Duke," said Buck hastily.

It was as though Buck Coulter was standing hat in hand before a superior, asking for charity rather than for what was due him. Duke didn't answer right away. He looked at Wes with thinly veiled contempt in his heavy-lidded eyes.

Buck jerked his head toward Wes. "The boy needs a loan, Duke," he said. "He knows *I'll* help him out."

Duke spat into a massive cuspidor. "You'll never get it back," he said. He tilted his head to look at Buck. "You finally run out your credit with Sophie Belaire?"

"For Christ's sake, Duke!" snapped Buck.

Duke smiled faintly as he reached inside his coat.

Wes was outright embarrassed. Duke wasn't acting as though dealing with his partner. What was it Buck had said? "I work *with* Duke Draegar, not *for* him." He saw Duke hold out a crisp one-hundred-dollar bill between two fingers as though he were handing out largess to a vassal. He was well nicknamed Duke. Then the man was gone into his sumptuous office, and the door closed behind him.

Buck turned and smiled. He stuffed the bill into Wes' shirt pocket. "On account, boy," he said. "I can't have Buck Coulter's friend wandering around Eden City like a saddle tramp."

"I'm not sure how soon I can pay you back," said Wes.

The gray eyes held Wes' eyes. "I am," said Buck quietly. He smiled. "I think you know what I mean. See you at ten o'clock." He limped back to his stool and climbed up into it.

Wes walked to the bar. He looked at the beer Curly had bought for him and then shoved it back. "Come on," he said. "I'd rather drink in a pig sty than this upholstered craphouse."

"Listen to him," murmured Anselmo.

Curly quickly drained Wes' beer and wiped his mouth. "It's your thirst," he said. "Come on!" He led the way to the door.

Wes eyed the bar as they walked past it. The mahogany was covered with glasses and money. "Money, money, money," said Wes. "It's all over this place like cowshit in a pasture, and ol' Wes Yardigan hasn't got a centavo of it, besides being in hock up to his skinny rump."

"Be patient, Wes," said Anselmo. He nodded knowingly.

"How long can you live on a legend?" said Wes dryly.

Curly stood beside his horse. "I'll go over to the Miner's Rest and get us a big room. They even got baths there. Me and Anselmo are all right, Wes, but *really,* you should *do* something about yourself. People are beginning to notice it."

"Gracias," said Wes. "Only a true friend would tell you."

"You and Anselmo take the horses and the burro to Brogan's Livery Stable," said Curly.

"Brogan's?" said Wes. "Is he still grubstaking Luke

39

Fairbairn in his hunt for Killdevil? Maybe Brogan doesn't know *we* have the key to the Lost Killdevil."

"For the love of God, Wes!" said Anselmo in a low voice. He looked hastily about them. "Do not say that name so carelessly here in Eden City! Times have changed since last you were here. It used to be a myth, a legend, as you say, but in the past year there has been strong talk that the place does exist and that a true *derrotero* has been seen here in town. There are many ears to listen, amigo. There are men who would kill for what we have."

Wes glanced sideways at Anselmo. "Yeh," he said quietly.

Anselmo looked away. "The Señor Wes is always the joker."

Curly cut through the thick traffic toward the Miner's Rest Hotel. Anselmo and Wes led the three horses and the burro east along Front Street. Eden City had boomed, thought Wes. Front Street was three times longer than when he had last been there. They turned from Main onto Yucca and walked toward the wide alleyway that led to Brogan's Livery Stable. There were some horses and burros in front of the open door of the stable. A man moved quickly through the pool of yellow light in front of the door. He wore a steeple-crowned Mex hat, banded with coin-silver ornamentation. Wes narrowed his eyes. There was something vaguely familiar about the man. The man disappeared inside the big, rambling livery stable. A man shouted, and then a woman screamed piercingly. Wes dropped the reins of the two horses he was leading and ran toward the stable. The woman screamed again. Somehow her voice was familiar.

FOUR

Wes closed in on the stable. A horse whinnied sharply. Wes glanced toward the horses and burros that stood outside the stable. One horse stood out from the others—a creamy-colored dun with a clearly recognizable black stripe down the middle of his back. "By Christ!" said Wes. "That's my dun!"

There was a struggle going on inside the stable. A man cursed fluently in gutter Spanish. The unmistakable sound of a hard fist striking flesh came to Wes. Wes almost forgot about the woman who had screamed. The sight of his dun had brought something else back to him, something that would be forever etched in his mind. The vivid memory of the Galeras Bunch and what they had done to him in the Lagarto filled him with a cold and bitter hate.

Wes jumped into the open doorway, cocked Colt at waist level, upper arm clamped to his side and the Colt swinging back and forth in a short arc to cover the men inside the stable. A broad-shouldered man wearing a charro jacket and a steeple hat banded with coin silver had an old man flat on his back in the muck of the stable floor, with one powerful brown hand clamped on the old man's throat beneath his flowing white beard. The old man's tongue was already protruding from between his stained yellow teeth. Beyond the two men was another Mexican, slim of build, struggling with a blonde young woman whose long hair fell across her face. Her dress had been ripped from shoulder to middle revealing her torn chemise and one of her breasts. The Mexican backhanded her even as Wes looked on.

"Lay off!" yelled Wes.

The big Mexican turned, freeing the old man and then ripping out a nickel-plated six-shooter from inside his jacket. He fired so fast that Wes hardly had time to leap to one side. The slug thudded into a post beside Wes. Wes fired, risking hitting the old man. "Get the hell outa the way, Luke!" yelled Wes even as he fired. The big slug caught the Mexican low in the guts. He crumpled forward, spasmodically firing his revolver. "Madre!" he cried once, and then he lay still.

Luke Fairbairn crawled weakly toward a stall, dragging his beard in the floor filth. Wreathing powder smoke swirled about Wes as he ran forward. A man yelled in the alleyway. The slim Mexican drew and fired as he released the young woman. Wes hit the ground, firing upward as he did so. Then he rolled sideways, and a slug struck the ground where he had been. The roaring discharges half deafened Wes. The Mexican grunted and staggered sideways, vainly trying to pull the young woman in front of him. She broke free and shoved the Mexican, sending him off balance. He went down on one knee just as Wes fired. The .44/40 slug caught him full in the throat. A gout of blood poured from his slack mouth as he pitched forward on his face. Wes ran toward the young woman. "Wes!" she screamed. "Watch your back!"

Wes whirled. A man stood in the doorway holding a Winchester at hip level. Wes fired a fraction of a second before he did. The impact of Wes' bullet drove the man backward, tilting up the rifle even as he fired. The rifle bullet smashed the lantern that hung from a post. Burning oil spewed from the shattered lantern and set fire to the litter on the stable floor. The fallen rifleman coughed once. It was the last sound he was ever to make.

"Madre de Dios!" yelled a man behind Wes. "He has killed Vito and Fedro! Gonzalo! Carl! To me! To me!"

Wes peered through the mingled smoke of lantern and gun. A Mexican was framed in the rear doorway. A thin scar marked his right cheek. "Luis Galeras!" yelled Wes. "You murderin' sonofabitch!" Wes fired but Luis Galeras had leaped aside and vanished from the doorway.

"Vamanos!" yelled the Mexican. "Pronto! He peddles too much death this night!" Boots thudded outside of the livery stable.

Wes wiped the sweat from his face as he felt for fresh cartridges. He flipped open the loading gate and ejected the hot brass hulls. He reloaded swiftly as he walked toward the rear door. There was hellfire in his eyes.

"Christ's Blood!" yelled Anselmo from the front doorway. "Have you not had enough killing for this night? Three dead men in three minutes by the clock!"

Wes stopped in his stride and slowly turned. He looked almost unseeingly at the white-faced Mexican. "I haven't finished yet," he said.

"Don't go, Wes!" cried Lucy. "They'll kill you!"

Wes slowly lowered the hot Colt. "No," he said. "They

won't kill me. Not tonight, anyway." He sheathed the weapon and picked up a tarp. He began to beat out the flames. He looked at Anselmo. "Shake the dung!" he roared. "Go get water!"

Pat Brogan ran into the stable, unsteady in his stride. "Holy Mother!" he yelled. "A man laves his stable for ten minutes to wet his throstle and comes back to a bloody massacre and a flaming holocaust to boot!"

Wes grinned crookedly. "You can't even spell it, Brogan," he said.

"Lookit me business!" yelled the Irishman.

"Go get a bucket, Shamrock," said Wes. "You're drunk."

The fire bell began to clang on Front Street. Men yelled as they ran toward the smoking stable. A bucket brigade was hastily formed, and water began to splash over the flames. Wes threw the tarp to one side and looked at Lucy. "You look just fine, Lucy," he said.

She had hastily pinned the front of her ruined dress together and had swept her thick hair back from her face. "I wish I could say the same for you," she said.

He raised his eyebrows. "Do I look that bad?" he asked.

She studied him. "It isn't that," she said quietly. "You kill awfully fast, Wes. Don't you feel anything at all?"

Wes shrugged. "Not for scum such as them. They left me to die out on the Lagarto. They might have killed all three of us tonight, and I assure you, Lucy, it wouldn't have bothered them at all. They left *me* to die. I came in time to kill *them*. It's justice, I suppose."

"The Mosaic Law," she said.

He nodded. "An eye for an eye; a tooth for a tooth. In my book, a life for a life. The blood debt."

"A hard law," she said.

"It's a hard country," he said. Their eyes met and held for a second or two, and then she looked away, and Wes Yardigan knew then that things hadn't changed much as far as Lucy Fairbairn was concerned. Maybe he should have stayed out on the Lagarto after all.

She looked beyond him, and her face changed. "You," she said in a tone of mingled disgust and fear.

Wes looked over his shoulder. Anselmo was standing there, with one eye fixed on Luke Fairbairn and the other wandering around in its own little private orbit. Lucy walked quickly over to her grandfather and knelt in the filth at his side. The old man opened his eyes and saw Anselmo. "Get away from me, greaser," he rasped in his thin voice. He clenched his fists and shook them at Anselmo.

Wes looked at Anselmo. "You seem to have the same happy effect on everyone you come in contact with, Anselmo," he said. "Go get the marshal."

"He's here," said Brogan from the doorway.

Buck Coulter limped into the smoke-filled stable. He glanced at the two dead Mexicans. "You sure peddle death in a hurry, boy," he said casually.

"I had a good instructor," said Wes.

A faint smile fled across Buck's face.

"It was self-defense, Marshal," said Brogan.

Buck nodded. "Obviously." He looked at Luke Fairbairn. "Are you all right, Luke?"

Luke sat up with the help of Lucy. He nodded. "No thanks to you, Coulter," he said.

Buck seemed a little annoyed. "I can't be everywhere in this town," he said.

Luke nodded. "Yup," he said. "Especially when you got work to do for Duke Draegar, eh?"

Buck flushed. "You always did talk too much, Luke," he said coldly.

Lucy eyed the marshal. "Maybe he doesn't talk enough," she said.

Buck raised his hat. "The fair sex is heard from," he said politely. "Do you represent the ladies of Eden City, ma'am?"

Lucy looked away. "No," she said. "They've done enough talking about you lately. I don't want to add to it."

It was a blow that cut across Buck's sensitiveness like a penitential lash. Wes couldn't help but feel sorry for him, but again the feeling came over him that Buck Coulter was not the same man he had been in years past. Buck looked about the stable. "You've learned to sharpen your

44

tongue, young lady," he said quietly. "Don't believe everything your grandfather says about me."

Lucy helped her grandfather to his feet. She did not answer the marshal. Wes gripped the old man by an arm. "I'll give you a hand to your quarters," he said. The old man looked suspiciously up at Wes. "You one of them?" he asked in a low voice.

Wes misunderstood him. "The Galeras Bunch? Not exactly, Luke. I wouldn't have much standing as a member after tonight."

The old man shook his head. "Not them," he said. He looked back at Buck and Anselmo. "I mean *them!*"

"I'm my own man," said Wes.

Luke looked up at Wes again. "I hope to God you are, son. I just hope to God you are!"

"Grandfather, be quiet," warned Lucy.

Wes looked toward the front doorway. People had massed in the alleyway. There was no sympathy in their eyes for the dead men. Anglo-Saxon eyes. Americans. Yankees and Southerners, perhaps but still *Americans.* There were no Latins in that curious crowd. Any Mexicans who might have been in the vicinity had swiftly faded out of the neighborhood. These cold-eyed Yanqui killers only counted a tally when they killed one of their own kind. Greasers and Indians didn't count.

Buck hooked a boot toe under the broad-shouldered Mexican. "Fedio Martinez," he said. "He's been long overdue for a killing." He glanced at the slim Mexican. "Vito Galeras. He has already earned a killing."

Anselmo jerked his head toward the dead man in the doorway. "Jim Lascomb," he said.

Buck relighted his cigar. "Half white and half nigger and all bad," he said. He fanned out the match. "Self-defense, I'd say. Coroner's inquest should cover this. No need to hold you, Wes." He turned. "Brogan! Get some of the boys to help you clean up this trash. Take them to Hastings Funeral Parlor. Tell John Hastings the burials are on me. We'll need a report from the coroner. Someone find him and sober him up long enough to make his examination. He can leave it in my office."

The three stiffening bodies were dumped into a buckboard. Anselmo picked up the rifle dropped by the man who had been killed in the doorway. "This looks familiar," he said.

Wes nodded. "You ought to know," he said. "I used it to run you out of my canyon not too long ago." He took it from the hands of the Mexican and looked at it. "Funny," he added. "I almost got it from my own rifle." He walked back to Lucy and the old man. "Where do you stay?" he asked.

"Beyond the corral," said Lucy. "On Bartlett Street. Pat Brogan lets us use his cottage when we're in town."

Wes took the old man by the arm. Luke swayed unsteadily. He pulled his arm away from Wes. "I can make it on my own," he said. Wes eyed him. Luke walked toward the door, and Wes caught him just before he fell. Wes swung him up and across his shoulders. "Show me the way, Lucy," he said.

"I'll be expecting you at ten," said Buck.

"I'll be there," said Wes. He did not see Buck hold Anselmo back by an arm and then shake his head.

Lucy led the way across the corral and opened a back gate into the small, weedy, and littered yard of a frame cottage that faced onto seedy Bartlett Street. She opened the back door of the cottage and quickly lighted an Argand lamp that stood on the kitchen table. She picked it up and led the way into the small living room. Wes placed Luke on a horsehair sofa.

"How is he?" Lucy asked anxiously.

Wes tilted back Luke's head and swept the thick beard to one side. The old man's throat still showed the impress of the Mexican's fingers. "He can talk," said Wes. "He'll be all right."

"Take mor'n a damned greaser to stop me from talkin'," snapped Luke.

Wes hunkered back on his heels and took out the makings. He looked at Lucy, and she nodded. "Sure, sure," said Wes. "By Godfrey, Luke, you just about had him, didn't you?" He shaped a cigarette, trying to keep a straight face.

"Let him alone," Lucy said sharply.

Wes stood up and lighted the cigarette from the lamp. "What was it all about?" he asked.

"They were after Lucy," said the old man. "Go get me a glass of brandy, Granddaughter."

"Do you think you should?" asked Lucy.

"Listen to her!" said the old man.

Lucy shrugged. She went into the kitchen. Luke struggled up into a sitting position. He eyed Wes. "So you've throwed in with them, eh, Wes?"

Wes twirled a chair about and straddled it, rested his crossed arms on the back of it, and eyed the old man through a thin wraith of tobacco smoke. "How did you figure that one out, Luke?" he said.

The sharp blue eyes studied Wes. "I don't have to have it written out for me," said Luke.

"You're lying like hell when you say they were after Lucy," said Wes.

"You ain't very gallant," said Luke.

Wes blew a smoke ring and punched a finger through it. "You still fool enough to be chasing after the Lost Killdevil?"

Luke lay down again. "Are *you*?" he said. "You didn't come out of the Lagarto just to show up in Brogan's Livery Stable in time to kill some scum."

"I'll admit that," said Wes.

"Look, son," said Luke quietly. "I know Buck Coulter is aimin' to go after the Lost Killdevil. You can copper *that* bet!"

Lucy brought in a tray with a bottle and two glasses on it. "Baconora, Wes," she said. "Unless your taste has changed."

He shook his head as he watched her fill the glasses. Lucy *had* changed. He touched the shirt pocket, where he kept the photograph of her. She had changed the image he had kept with him all those lonely months out on the Lagarto.

"We can talk in front of her," said Luke.

"I wasn't aiming to keep anything from Lucy," said Wes.

She handed him his glass. "I'm not sure I want to hear anything, Wes. Isn't it always the same with you? Lost

47

mines and big strikes. Bonanza! The Mother Lode! Did you come back from the Lagarto as a rich man to impress Eden City with your wealth?"

Wes whistled softly. "Listen to her!" he said.

She tapped a foot on the floor. "Well?" she said.

Luke downed his drink and held out the glass for a refill. "I was tellin' Wes here that Buck Coulter and his two associates, those sterling characters Curly Killigrew and Anselmo Abeyta, were after the Killdevil."

"He knows that," she said quietly. "Isn't that why you came back from the Lagarto, Wes?"

He nodded. He sipped his drink and looked at her over the rim of the glass. "Why not?" he said.

"You wouldn't leave the Lagarto for me, though, would you?"

"You really didn't ask me to, Lucy," he said.

"Do you have to be told everything?" she snapped.

Wes looked down at his drink. "It might have helped," he said quietly. "I didn't find a lost mine in the Lagarto, or a bonanza. I didn't come back to Eden City to impress anyone." He looked up at her. "But what I learned those long months alone on the Lagarto might be worth more than any bonanza."

"Listen to him!" jeered Luke. "A saddle tramp without a centavo to his name goes into the Lagarto and months later he comes back. What do we get? A damned philosopher! That's what!"

Wes grinned. "Hell, Luke," he said. "You can't even spell the word let alone tell anyone what it means."

"Maybe so! But I can tell you I don't like it!"

Wes waved his glass and drained it. Lucy refilled it. She came so close that her breasts touched his shoulder, and he remembered all too clearly seeing her struggling in the dimly lit stable with one firm, rounded breast swinging freely. Maybe they *had* been after Lucy after all. A languorous warmth crept through his belly and up into his chest. He wasn't sure whether it was from contact with Lucy or from the brandy, or maybe both. He saw Luke's keen blue eyes on him. The old devil seemed to be able to look right through a man into his inner thoughts.

Wes didn't wait for Luke to speak. He moved into the attack. "What were the Galeras boys after?" he said.

"You aimin' to throw in with Buck Coulter?" asked Luke.

"You keep saying that," said Wes. "I didn't say it."

"You didn't say you wasn't!"

Wes stood up and placed the glass on the tray. "I didn't come here to argue with you, you old catamount," he said.

Luke sat up and pointed a finger at Wes. "I know all about it!" he rasped. "I know how Buck Coulter got ahold of them pieces of *derrotero*!"

Wes looked down at him. "You're doing an awful lot of talking, old man, and you're not making a damned bit of sense. What *derrotero*?"

Luke looked at Lucy. "Listen to him!" he jeered. "Wes knows what I mean! Look at him! He knows what I mean!" Luke turned. "No use trying to pull the wool over my eyes, Wes. I know Buck Coulter has two pieces of the true *derrotero* to the Lost Killdevil. The *derrotero* made by old Jesus Melgosa hisself! I know, mister, because I saw it years ago when Jesus showed it to Eusebio Ochoa."

Wes laughed. "You're killing me," he said. "If Eusebio Ochoa had seen that *derrotero*, he would have found the Lost Killdevil."

Luke half closed his eyes. "Maybe he did," he said.

Wes felt cold all over. Even the good brandy could not fight the chill. "Impossible," he said at last.

"Maybe he did," repeated Luke. "And maybe he paid the price for finding it. The price the Espantosas sometimes ask for a man."

"You've had too much brandy along with that knock on the cabeza," said Wes.

Luke closed his eyes. "You know what I mean. Maybe that's the reason you stay away from around here. Lots of people wonder about Wes Yardigan and why he don't come back to his birthplace. Yeh, they wonder why he stays out on the Lagarto instead of gettin' a decent job like other folks."

"Like you," said Wes dryly. "When's the last time you had a steady job, you old sidewinder?"

"Maybe Eusebio Ochoa would still be alive, enjoyin' his riches, if you hadn't left the old man to go it alone."

Wes felt his jaw muscles tighten. "You always did talk too damned much," he said coldly. "Never think first about what you're going to say. Just open your mouth and drool it out."

Luke opened his eyes. "All I know is that no man should go into them mountains after the Lost Killdevil unless he's got someone *trustworthy* to back him. It ain't no place for a lone hand. My son Jim found that out." He looked suddenly at Lucy, and his face reddened. The young woman turned on a heel and left the room. Wes heard a faint sobbing coming from the kitchen, and then the back door opened and closed.

"Get to your point," said Wes.

"How did Buck Coulter get two pieces of the true *derrotero?*" said the old man, as though to himself.

"I'll have to admit I was wondering about that myself," said Wes. The old man knew well enough that Buck had the two pieces of *derrotero* and that Wes had thrown in with Buck Coulter and the others. Wes emptied his glass and refilled it. The brandy had no effect upon him. It was always so after a killing. Taking the life of another man does not make a soft pillow at night.

Luke drained his glass, wiped his mouth and beard, and looked owlishly at Wes. "Eusebio Ochoa had a piece of the true *derrotero* with him when he was murdered in the Espantosas. My son Jim had another piece of the true *derrotero* when he was murdered in the Espantosas. Neither piece of *derrotero* was found with the bodies."

"You could hardly expect that," Wes said dryly.

Luke looked past Wes as though the wall of the room had disappeared and he could see the distant Espantosas. "There was a young Mexican who went with my Jim when he went into the Espantosas to hunt for Killdevil. Marcos Padilla loved my son. When Jim was murdered, Marcos fled from those accursed mountains. Buck Coulter picked up Marcos here in Eden City on a drunk charge, but the boy never drank. He was half out of his mind with fear. He babbled something about the death of Jim, but Buck Coulter was the only one who heard what the boy said. Buck jailed him on suspicion of murder. No one was on duty in the jail that night. Buck was too busy with his other jobs. The next morning they found Marcos Padilla hanging by his belt in his cell." The old man's voice died away. He seemed to come back into the room again from the distant Espantosas.

"Go on," said Wes.

Luke looked at Wes. "Shortly thereafter Buck Coulter has two pieces of the true *derrotero*." Luke half closed his eyes. "Odd, isn't it? Buck had never shown any interest in the Lost Killdevil before that time. Too busy making money, or so they say."

"You're making some damned dangerous accusations," said Wes as he lighted a cigarette.

Luke smiled shrewdly. "Who? *Me*?" He waved a heavily veined hand.

"Where did Jim get his piece of the chart?" asked Wes.

"From Marcos Padilla," said Luke. "It is said, although no one knows for sure, that Marcos was a great-grandson of old Jesus Melgosa. In any case, the boy did have a piece of the javelina hide. I held it in these very hands. Jim would not have gone after the mine if I had not said that it looked as though the piece of *derrotero* was authentic. He wouldn't wait. He wouldn't let me go with him. It was too dangerous, he said." Luke closed his eyes and shook his head. "He needed me, Wes. God, how he needed me! I could have helped! I could have watched his back while he hunted. The Padilla boy was not one to do such duty in those cursed mountains."

"You speak only of two pieces," said Wes. "Where is the third and last piece?"

Luke opened his eyes, but they revealed nothing. "Quién sabe?" he said quietly.

"What's your game, Luke?" asked Wes.

Luke shook his head. "You're going along with Buck, Curly, and Anselmo, then?"

Wes nodded.

51

"Then, you aren't interested in my game," said Luke.

"What are you driving at?" Wes demanded.

Luke leaned forward. "Forget about Buck Coulter and his partnership, Wes. Throw in with me! I need your help."

"To what end?" said Wes.

"Gold," said Luke dreamily. "A fortune in gold."

Wes looked down at him. Old Luke had been looking for lost mines and rich lodes when he had been Young Luke and he'd never stop until he breathed his last or was too weak to carry on. "You're too old," Wes said quietly. "Forget it, Luke."

"You won't throw in with me and the girl?"

"Leave her out of it," said Wes.

Luke looked up at Wes. "I always suspected you were a damned fool," he said. "Now I know it!" He jerked his head toward the rear of the house. "You've got a greater fortune in that girl than you'll ever find in the Lagarto or them damned, bloody Espantosas. But you ain't got the sense to know that."

"I've got enough sense to warn you to stay away from the Espantosas yourself."

A moment or two ticked past. Luke rested his head back against the sofa. "Go on," he said quietly. "Go on with your three friends, Yardigan. Maybe you'll find the Lost Killdevil and maybe you'll find something else. Something that you might not expect to find." He raised his head. "You think any of those three will play the game square with you if they get sight of the Lost Killdevil? Don't fool yourself, mister! If I ever seen death in human form, I see it in their faces for anyone who crosses them. Go on! Get out of my sight!"

Wes picked up his hat and walked from the room. He crossed the kitchen and opened the rear door. Lucy stood beside the fence. She turned as he approached her. "Well?" she said. "Are you going with him?"

"I have an obligation to pay," he said.

She nodded. "I thought as much."

"Keep him away from those mountains," warned Wes.

"Nothing on earth can keep him away from those

52

mountains as long as he is alive," she said. "What is more, Wes, as long as he insists on going up there, I'm going with him."

"You're crazier than he is!" Wes said angrily.

"Gracias," she murmured.

For a moment he stood looking down at her, but there was nothing he could do or say to stop her from going into the Espantosas with the old man. He glanced back at the house. Yes, there *was* something he could do to stop her from going with the old man. That was to go himself with Luke Fairbairn.

She looked up at him with those great eyes of hers. "Buck Coulter is expecting you at ten," she said.

It was the moment of decision, the moment of truth.

"Wes?" she said.

Wes shook his head. "Good night, Lucy," he said. He strode across the littered yard and he did not look back. When he reached the far side of the livery stable corral, he did look back. She was gone. Once he attended the meeting with Buck, Anselmo, and Curly, he would be thoroughly committed to them. There would be no going back. The old man's words came back to him as he walked toward Front Street. *"Don't fool yourself, mister! If I ever seen death in human form, I see it in their faces for anyone who crosses them."*

FIVE

The Territorial House towered three storeys above Front Street at the corner of Prescott. Wes Yardigan had never been in the place in the old days. It had been far too elegant for a saddle bum like himself to enter without being too self-conscious. Now he didn't give a damn. His newly shaved face felt a little raw, and the boiled collar he wore felt like a wagon tire iron being shrunk onto a rim, but otherwise he felt fine enough. He had split a bottle of Baconora with Curly and Anselmo at the Miner's Rest and had left the two of them arguing drunkenly on whether to blow good money on the elegant whores of Prescott Street or to work along the line of two-bit cribs in Chile Town. Strangely enough, the good brandy had had little effect on Wes Yardigan. It was one of those days.

Wes opened the elegant cut glass door of the hotel and crossed the thickly carpeted lobby lined with luxuriant potted ferns and palms. He heard the tinkle of glass and metal dining ware from the dining room off the lobby. Buck sure lived in style. It hadn't been too many years past since Buck and Wes used to bunk down in Brogan's hayloft after a night of bar rounds.

"Mr. Coulter's room, please," said Wes to the slim young man who eyed him suspiciously and a little disdainfully from the other side of the counter.

"Suite Two-A," the young man said in a nasal tone. "The President Grant Suite."

Wes selected a cigar from the box on the counter and bit off the end. "That so?" he said. He snapped a lucifer into flame from a thumbnail and touched it to the tip of the cigar. "President Grant ever *see* it or sleep in it?" he asked between puffs. He dropped a quarter for the cigar onto the mahogany.

"Mr. Coulter has a guest at the moment," said the young man.

"That so?" murmured Wes. He *was* beginning to feel the brandy. "He's going to have another any minute."

"Be careful with those ashes!" snapped the clerk. "That rug was imported all the way from Kansas City."

"Do tell!" said Wes in awe. He leaned across the counter. "I've been imported all the way from the Lagarto Desierto and I don't give a good gawd-damn about your Kansas City rug, mister!" Wes walked toward the broad staircase.

"I'd like to know your name, mister!" the clerk called out.

Wes turned on the first step. "Yardigan," he said. "Wesley Duncan Yardigan, mister."

"Oh, my God," said the clerk in a small voice.

Wes was well up the stairway before he let the grin crack his freshly shaven face. "Word *does* get around," he

54

said to himself. How the hell does Buck pay his way in this classy place? thought Wes. Something kept running through his mind—Duke Draegar's attitude about a loan to Buck and his mentioning of Buck's being likely to run out of credit with Sophie Belaire. Yet Curly Killigrew had said that Buck owned a piece of the Buckhorn, and Anselmo Abeyta had said that Buck had set Sophie up in her new parlor house on Prescott Street. Something was almighty wrong someplace. Buck could certainly act as chief marshal of Eden City, for he was a professional lawman, likely the best in the Territory, but that didn't take any brains for business management. If it had, Buck Coulter couldn't have held down the star. On the other hand, if one were to select two top sets of business brains, albeit *shady* business, he'd have to search well and diligently throughout the Territory to top Duke Draegar and Sophie Belaire. "Begod," said Wes aloud. "Even *I've* got better business brains than Buck has." A woman laughed as Wes passed one of the many polished walnut doors. He solemnly tipped his new hat. "Must be his wife," he said. "After all, this *is* the Territorial House!"

The light from a highly polished Argand lamp set upon a marble-topped table in the hallway reflected dully from the brass plate on the walnut door of Number 2-A. Above the number a bust of President Grant had been etched in fine detail. "I wonder if he knows of this great honor," said Wes. He grinned. "Maybe I *am* getting drunk." He rapped on the door.

The door swung open. Buck Coulter stood there with a cigar in one hand and a half-full glass in the other and the winning Buck Coulter smile on his lean face. "By God," he said. "Right on time! You're learning, boy! You're learning!"

Wes grinned. "Your nasal friend down at the desk said you had a guest. I guess he figured I wasn't to disturb you."

Buck widened his eyes. "A guest?" He laughed. "He meant an old friend of yours, Wes. Look there!"

Wes looked beyond Buck. A woman was standing at one of the bay windows that looked down on Front Street. Wes recognized the shapely back and the lovely, piled-up

55

hair with the highlights in it. Sophie Belaire turned slowly and effectively. Her youthful beauty was fading slightly, but it was still enough to make a man's mind catch a little and lose the routined, disciplined step of it. Her wide green eyes surveyed Wes a little cooly. "How are you, Wes?" she said in the self-trained, well-modulated voice that had no trace left in it of the Chicago "Back-of-the-Yards" Polack. She had at least a good ten years on Wes, but she could still shake a man's soul and reason with those emerald eyes, creamy skin, soft, full mouth, and hourglass figure that didn't seem, at least to Wes Yardigan, to be much hampered by those binding things women favored around their busts and hips.

"Watch it, Soph," said Buck. "Wes has been out on the Lagarto too long! Don't take any chances! I know how it is! After the first month the saguaros begin to look like women standing there in the moonlight, and when you finally get around to propositioning one of them, you've been out on the Lagarto *too* long, brother!"

Sophie tilted her lovely head to one side and studied Wes. "You've changed, Wes," she said thoughtfully.

Buck drained his glass. "Wes maybe isn't feeling too cheerful, Sophie," he said. "Killed three men tonight."

Her eyes half closed. "I heard about it," she said softly. "It was about a woman, wasn't it, Wes?"

Wes took off his hat and placed it on a table. "Lucy Fairbairn," he said quietly. He didn't want to look at her.

"My God, Wes! Is *that* still on!"

Wes shook his head. "They were working over the old man."

"The Galeras Bunch," she said.

He looked sideways at her. "You get all the fresh news, Sophie," he said.

She smiled thinly. "That's all in my line of business, Wes. Sometimes we get the news *before* it happens. The things I could tell you about the honorable citizens of Eden City—and, by God, the whole damned Territory!"

"Take it easy, Soph," said Buck. "What's your pleasure, Wes?"

Wes glanced at the ranked bottles on the side table. "Rye ought to work," he said.

Buck grinned. "Brandy working off, eh?"

Wes shook his head. "Just laid a foundation is all, Buck. I see you've taken the pledge."

Buck dropped his glass and slapped a hand on the table. "You crazy sonofabitch!" he roared. "By God, I've missed you and that damned dry humor of yours!"

Wes relighted his cigar. "Careful," he warned. "They's a lady present, Buck."

Sophie tilted her head to one side. "Why don't you go plumb to hell, you saddle tramp!" she snapped.

Wes fanned out the match. "Sounds like old times," he murmured. "Sorry, Sophie." He did not dare look at her.

"Take it easy, Soph," said Buck as he handed Wes a glass. "Wes and I have some business to talk about," he added suggestively.

"I know," she said. "The Lost Killdevil."

Wes looked at her. "She knows about this deal, too?" he said over his shoulder to Buck.

"You damned well know it!" she said.

Wes looked at Buck. "No one told me about this part of it."

Buck flushed a little. "Well, me and Sophie have a deal, too," he said.

"Like what?" said Wes coldly.

Buck coughed a little as he lowered his glass. "Damned stuff bites well," he said appreciatively. He would not look directly at Wes. "Might be wedding bells for the two of us if I can make a killing with the Killdevil." He walked to the window and looked down on the street.

Wes sipped the strong liquor. What a combination! Buck Coulter, the Living Legend of Arizona Territory, and Sophie Belaire, the Classiest Calico Cat west of the Mississippi. "By God," he said as he lowered his glass. "Now I have seen the elephant!"

"What Mr. Coulter means, Mr. Yardigan," Sophie said precisely, "is that *I* get a fifth share of the deal."

Wes swirled the liquor in his glass. "I can just see *you* in a huck shirt and a pair of dirty levis riding a jackass

57

through those mountains looking for a lost gold mine. Isn't there enough easy gold for you on Prescott Street, Soph?" He looked directly at her. The lovely emerald eyes had changed into glittering chips of green glass.

"She's in on the deal," snapped Buck as he turned and looked at Wes. "It's all right with Curly and Anselmo."

"Maybe it's not all right with me," said Wes.

It was very quiet in the big room. The wind stirred the curtains, and the faint sound of voices drifted up from the street. Wes placed his half-empty glass on the table. He looked from one to the other of them, and the odd thought drifted through his mind that one of them might be just as dangerous as the other if crossed.

"You're not making sense," said Buck in a low voice. "Don't you believe in the Lost Killdevil? Didn't you see that piece of *derrotero?* What do you think of that, eh?"

"It *looks* authentic," Wes admitted.

"What the hell do you mean by that?" snapped Sophie. "I thought you were the expert."

"He is," said Buck. He walked toward her and touched her smooth white shoulder. As he kissed her rounded neck he whispered something to her. She raised her head and looked once again at Wes, but the cold dislike in her look didn't shake Wes Yardigan one bit, although he wasn't sure but what it was the mingled brandy and rye that was making him so all-fired unconcerned about the feeling Sophie Belaire had for him.

Buck slipped her fashionable paletot coat over her shoulders and helped her as she slid her arms into the sleeves. He looked past her at Wes and shook his head. Wes drained his glass and refilled it. He did not look up as they walked together to the door and out into the hall. The door clicked shut behind them, and he immediately heard her voice rise in pitch. "That sonofabitch!" she said. "Who the hell does he think he is?" Wes could hear Buck's low voice.

Wes walked to the window and stood there looking down into the street until he heard the door open and close behind him. He did not turn as he heard Buck filling a glass. It was Buck's gambit. He could throw the game either way by what he was about to say.

58

"Now ain't *she* the bitch-kitty?" Buck said dryly.

Wes turned his head. "You said it, Buck. I didn't. Remember that when you sober up."

Buck raised his glass and eyed the liquor in the lamplight. "I'm not drunk, boy," he said quietly. He lowered the glass and studied Wes.

"How did she get into the deal?"

Buck dropped heavily into a wing chair and idly swirled the liquor in his glass. "She comes high, boy," he said in a low voice.

Wes sat down and studied Buck. "You said wedding bells. You were joking, of course."

Buck shook his head. He emptied his glass. "You don't joke about things like that with Sophie Balaire."

"You love her, I assume."

Buck looked up. "You assume shit, amigo!"

"Then, I don't get it, Buck."

Buck took Wes' glass from his hand and limped over to the table. "It was a business deal I made with her. I messed it up. That's all."

"You always had a great business head," said Wes.

Buck flushed. "Take it easy, Wes."

"Well it's the goddamned truth, isn't it?"

Buck filled the glasses and handed one to Wes. "You've got me there, boy," he admitted.

"What the hell has happened to you in this sinkhole? Curly and Anselmo gave me a big buildup about you being partners with Duke Draegar. About setting Sophie Belaire up in her new cathouse. About being chief marshal of Eden City. I saw how Duke spoke to you in the Buckhorn, and it made my guts turn over! I heard what he said about you running out your credit with Sophie Belaire. You didn't take *that* too well, even if you were touching up Duke for a century note for me. I heard how Luke Fairbairn—and Lucy, for that matter—spoke to you in Brogan's."

Buck waved his cigar. "Old Luke is completely hillnutty. Lucy believes everything he tells her."

"Maybe," said Wes quietly. "But what about the other things I just said?"

Buck's hand closed tightly on his whiskey glass, and the

59

knuckles stood out whitely against the brown skin. "You always did talk too goddamned much," he said.

"Granted," said Wes. "Now, ease up on that glass, or you'll ruin the fastest gun hand in the Territory."

Buck looked down at the glass as though seeing it for the first time. "Jesus," he said softly. "If a man could just go back and undo some things."

"Forget it," said Wes. "Look, Buck! You can fool some of these clods and get away with it, but that's not your style. You can tell me the truth at least. Put up the sham for the public but not for Wes Yardigan. The fact is that you're busted and you're in hock up to your ass to boot with Duke Draegar and Sophie Belaire and God-alone-knows-who-else. You knew when you sent for me that you had just about run out your string. Why in hell's name can't you tell me the truth?"

Buck hesitantly raised his head, and the fine gray eyes held those of Wes. "You know something, boy?" he said quietly. "Whether or not you throw in with me on the Killdevil isn't as important to me right now as the fact that you came all the way from the Lagarto to talk to old Buck."

Wes grinned. "Bullshit! I was dead broke out there and damned near about to cash in my chips when the boys came after me. I didn't mind you sending ol' Curly Killigrew, but why'd you have to send that shifty-eyed killer Anselmo along with him."

Buck drained his glass. "Well, it was like this, boy—I knew you'd have confidence in ol' Anselmo."

"How so?"

Buck grinned. "Why, you silly sonofabitch, can't you figure that one out? If Anselmo didn't shoot you in the back or stab you for your poke, it was a lead pipe cinch he was there on more important business."

Wes leaned back in his chair. "There always was a touch of the genius about you, Buck," he said in admiration.

"Me and you together," said Buck complacently. "The only two damned geniuses in the whole Territory of Arizona. Right?"

"Right!" said Wes.

"You'll drink on that?"

"You twisted my arm."

They raised glasses and clinked them together and downed the rye. Buck wiped his mouth and looked thoughtfully at Wes. "Like I said, the only two geniuses in the Territory, but lately I've been damned suspicious of you, boy."

"You have the subtle approach, amigo."

Buck leaned back in the chair. "What about it, boy?"

"The Killdevil?"

"What else is there to talk about?"

Wes nodded. "You don't think the Killdevil is just a legend, then? A myth? A lie that grew with the years into the status of a legend?"

"No, I don't," said Buck evenly, "and what is more, neither do you."

Wes could not meet his gaze. He emptied his glass. The rye and the brandy made a curious, warming, devil-may-care combination in his gut. Take it easy, he thought. Don't let the booze do the talking and for God's sake don't fall for the Buck Coulter charm.

"You always planned one day to go into the Espantosas and find that mine," said Buck. He picked up his heavy cane and began to twirl it in his fingers like a drum major. "You weren't out on the Lagarto to pick dewberries, sonny."

"You know a helluva lot," said Wes.

"More booze?"

Wes shook his head.

"Give me the glass. You know well enough I wouldn't make any drunken deals with you."

Wes handed him the glass. He watched Buck fill the glasses. He leaned back in his chair and looked around the comfortable room. Buck did himself well. Wes wondered how much past rent Buck owed. It would have been beyond Wes to stay in such a place without a pair of silver eagles to rub together in his pants pocket—but, then, Wes wasn't Buck Coulter. Still, with the take from the Killdevil a man could live like a king, for a time, at least, if he wasn't smart enough to take his share and beat it to hell out of Eden City like the devil beating tanbark.

61

Buck handed him his glass. "You aimin' to be a saddle bum all your life?" he asked.

"It's not so bad," said Wes.

"You're a damned liar! You like the nice things, boy, and the only reason you don't go after them is because you want to be able to pay for them before you use them up. God's blood! Curly said you even read books now!"

Wes laughed. "Condemned in his eyes forever."

Buck grinned. "That's about the size of it." He began to untwist the heavy silver cap on top of his ebony stick. He took it off and shook out something that looked familiar to Wes. Rolled javelina hide, scraped as thin as parchment. Two pieces of it lay on the table. "Anselmo brought up the second piece whilst you were soaking in the tub over at the Miner's Rest," said Buck.

"I could have brought it over," said Wes.

"Yeh," said Buck thoughtfully.

Wes did not press the subject. "I want you to know that even if you let me see those two pieces together, that's no contract with me to go with you."

"I didn't say that," said Buck. He looked sideways at Wes. "I'm not worried about you, boy." There was the faintest hint of warning in his low voice. "Go ahead. Take a look. A *long* look."

Wes spread out the two thin pieces of hide and fitted the edges together. He rested his hands on either side of the chart and began to study it under the bright light of the table lamp. He oriented the *derrotero* from the clearly indicated position of Sangre Cuchillo Peak and the Eye of Death at its northeastern base. The Eye of Death was one of the few all-season water holes in the Espantosas. One marking had almost been destroyed where the thin hide had been torn apart. It looked like something familiar, but he couldn't be sure. If it was what he thought it might be ... He stored the thought in the dormant file of his mind for later reference. It wasn't possible, but all the same it was something to consider.

"Well?" said Buck at last.

Wes did not look up. "It looks authentic," he said cautiously.

"Go on, boy."

"What you've got here, as closely as I can figure, is the start of a chart to find the Lost Killdevil. You need the missing piece, or pieces, to complete the search."

Buck shifted in his seat and sipped his drink. "You mean that whoever has the missing piece or pieces can find the mine?"

Wes shrugged. "It isn't likely. They've got the end, and you have the beginning and the middle, so to speak. They'd likely have to have these two pieces to know where to start the search." He laughed dryly. "And you need theirs to end the search. You need whoever has it for another partner, Buck."

It was very quiet in the room. A moth bumbled about a lamp near the window. A door slammed down the hallway. A piece of ice shifted in the glass bowl on the table.

"Could you figure out the ending if we worked with what we now have?" said Buck at last.

Wes shrugged again. He began to shape a cigarette. "Eusebio Ochoa might have done it," he said.

"Eusebio Ochoa is dead, Wes."

Wes lighted the quirley from the top of the lamp cylinder. He watched the smoke lift and waver in the updraft and then drift toward the open window.

"Eusebio Ochoa is dead," continued Buck, "but his memory did not die with him. Wes, you are probably the only living man who can interpret that *derrotero*. Am I right?"

Wes rubbed his clean-shaven face and looked down at the ancient *derrotero*. The damned thing had a lure to it, even lying on a marble-topped table in the best suite in the Territorial House in Eden City. It had a lure that drew Wes into its grip, and he knew he had to go back into the Espantosas. It was as Anselmo had said: "It is said that one must always come back to them, is that not so, Wes?"

"Wes, is it authentic?" Buck asked.

"Yes," said Wes quietly. "I think it is."

"By Christ! That's good enough for me!"

Wes looked at him. "How did you happen to get these two pieces, Buck?"

"Is that important?"

"It is—to *me.*"

"Anselmo's sainted grandfather left him one piece," said Buck.

Wes rolled his eyes upward. "Jesus Christ!" he said.

It didn't faze Buck Coulter—not at all. "Jim Fairbairn was murdered by a young Mexican, name of Marcos Padilla, up in the Espantosas. I picked up Padilla a few days after the killing. He was half out of his mind. Deathly afraid of someone. Maybe it was Old Luke. You know how he is."

"Yeh," said Wes dryly. "I know how he is."

Buck lighted a fresh cigar and puffed it into life. "Padilla hung himself in his cell. Saved the county a hanging. Padilla held nothing against me for arresting him. Left me all his possessions. One of those possessions was that left-hand piece there of the *derrotero*. The kid didn't have a living soul as relative. He wrote out his will on a piece of paper. I have the paper in my office safe if you'd like to see it."

Wes shook his head. If it was a whopper, it was a dandy. "Maybe the piece of *derrotero* belonged to Jim Fairbairn, Buck."

Buck shook his head. "Not likely."

"But you don't really know, do you?"

Buck inspected the end of his cigar. "I've got as much right to that piece of hide as anyone has. If you don't like the deal, you can pull out right now, Wes."

Wes walked to the window and looked out at the dark sky. Maybe Buck was telling the full truth. Possession was nine-tenths of the law, or so it was said. Who could prove otherwise? Where had Anselmo Abeyta really gotten the other piece of *derrotero*? Luke Fairbairn had hinted broadly enough that Eusebio Ochoa had had a piece of the *derrotero* when he, too, had been murdered in the Espantosas. *"Everyone knew Eusebio Ochoa had a piece of the true derrotero. It was not found with his body,"* Luke had said.

"The odds are with us," said Buck.

Wes was almost startled. He had been woolgathering, a bad habit he had acquired in the Lagarto Desierto.

"Maybe the Espantosas bother you too much," suggested Buck.

"Mountains are mountains," said Wes dryly.

"I've arranged for everything," said Buck. "Picks, spades, grub, rope, lanterns—the whole bit, boy. We can slip out of Eden City one by one and rendezvous near Tonto Seep. Anselmo will bring along a pack burro with the heavier gear. All you have to do is say you'll go."

Wes flipped his cigarette butt out of the window and watched it trail sparks until it hit the rutted street below. "You forgot one thing, amigo," he said over his shoulder.

"I haven't forgotten one damned thing, boy."

Wes grinned. "Dumb luck," he said. He turned. "You saving all that good liquor for a sick friend?"

Buck shook his head in relief. "Damn you," he said. "You almost had me there, Wes."

Wes eyed him. "You knew all the time I'd throw in with you," he said.

"It will be like old times, eh, Wes?" said Buck eagerly. His lean face lighted up. "By God! We'll make it! We never blew a job yet and we aren't about to start now."

"There's one thing, Buck," said Wes.

"Name it!" said Buck expansively.

"If Luke Fairbairn goes up into the Espantosas, I want him left alone."

Buck was startled. "Who was going to bother that loco old coot?" His eyes narrowed. "What the hell did he say to you about me?"

"Nothing."

Buck studied Wes. "All right, boy. I wasn't intending Old Luke any harm, but if it makes you feel better, I'll agree to leave him alone. Does that include the Galeras Bunch as well?"

Wes grinned. "Now, wouldn't it be just something, say, if those coyotes came into the Espantosas looking for trouble? Makes a man feel all loose and warm inside, just like a kid on Christmas morning."

Buck nodded. "Like the time we caught Cass Moxon and his outfit at Pipe Spring."

"It was Dragoon Spring," said Wes.

Buck limped to the table and filled the glasses. "Jesus, but the bullets were flying that day, eh, Wes?"

"A man could have swung a tin cup into the air and filled it with slugs in about a minute," agreed Wes.

Buck shook his head. "You know, Wes, I never told you this, but I didn't think we would make it that day. Damn, but a man had sheer dumb luck to get through that."

"Shit," said Wes. "We were just *good,* amigo."

Buck handed him his glass, and they both sat down. Neither of them spoke for a time. Buck looked up. "Was it as bad as we make it out be be, boy?"

Wes shrugged. "It was pretty bad. Scared the bejasus out of me, I tell you. Funny thing—all the time the bullets were buzzing like bees in a hive, I kept thinking about a nursery rhyme my mother used to sing. Ring around a rosey, a pocketful of posies. Achoo! Achoo! All fall down!"

It was very quiet in the room. The tobacco smoke rifted and wavered over their heads. Buck looked at Wes. "You figure we'll make it this time, boy?"

"We can try," said Wes. He swirled the liquor in his glass. He was beginning to feel it now, at last. It was a good feeling. "You really aim to marry Sophie, Buck?"

Buck nodded.

"You really love her, then?"

"I didn't say that."

"Then you're a double-damned fool. Look, Buck, if we make this strike, you can pay off your debts. Hell! You can use part of my share if you like. Anything to get you free of this sinkhole! Look here! There's a spread up near the Chiricahuas. Good grazing, plenty of water, winter shelter, streams full of trout, and hills full of game. A man could live like a king there, Buck! A few thouand maybe could carry it on time, and a couple of good men like ourselves could make it pay off, I tell you. What do you say?"

Buck looked up and stuck out a powerful hand. "Boy, you've got yourself a deal! First we hit the ol' Killdevil and clean it out and then we head for those Chiricahua hills to see what is what. We'll drink on that, eh?"

Wes grinned. "Why not? We've been drinking on everything else tonight. Might as well keep on."

"I've got midnight rounds coming up, boy, otherwise we'd put on a real bender and end up sleeping in old Brogan's hayloft like we used to, with the mice running over us getting drunker by the minute after smelling our breaths."

It was quarter to twelve when two happy, but slightly drunken men came down the stairway into the elegant lobby of the Territorial House. The clerk eyed them as they weaved a little in their purposeful stride. "Careful of the gawd-damned rug, Marshal Coulter," said Wes. "It came plumb all the way from Kansas City. Some sodbuster used it for a wagon cover and sold it to the Territorial House when he got here as a real, genuine *Eastern* antique."

"You won't join me on my rounds?" said Buck when they reached the street.

"They'll think you've picked up another drunk," said Wes.

Buck nodded. "A man is known by the company he keeps."

"And the pig got up and slowly walked away."

"Exactly," said Buck. He looked to the northeast to where the clear moonlight was gilding the upper ramparts of the Espantosas. The sharp tip of Sangre Cuchillo Peak stood out like a warning finger, or a beckoning one, depending upon the way a man felt about the Espantosas. "What's up there for us, hey, boy?" said Buck quietly. His eyes seemed to glitter a little in the moonlight, maybe with excitement, maybe from too much good rye whiskey. "A fortune for us? A whole future? What do you think, boy?"

Wes rolled a cigarette. He nodded. "I think we'll make it, Buck. We *have* to make it."

Buck looked sideways at him. "Yes," he said quietly. "We have to make it, don't we? Good night, Wes."

Wes snapped a lucifer into flame and lighted the cigarette. He watched Buck limping across the intersection, his silver-tipped cane swinging and shining in the moonlight. By God and all that was holy, there went a *man!*

Wes walked slowly toward his hotel. He was tired, and the rye would drug him to sleep. He turned once more before he entered the hotel. It was a warm night in early fall, but as he studied those brooding and mysterious mountains bathed in that cold and eerie light an icy fingertip seemed to trace the whole length of his spine.

SIX

Wes Yardigan lay belly-flat on the reverse slope of the ridge that overlooked Tonto Canyon. To his right, far down the rocky slope, was the clump of greenery that marked Tonto Seep, but it was shielded in thick darkness. The first faint promise of the false dawn touched the eastern sky, but the great bulk of the Espantosas were still in darkness. Wes lay with his bare head amid a clump of bear grass. He sure could have used a smoke. He looked back over his shoulder and down the reverse slope. A faint pinpoint of light sparked up now and then. One of his three companions was sneaking a smoke. If the wind shifted, the odor of the smoke might be picked up by anyone riding the trail eastward from Tonto Seep. It wouldn't be Buck who was smoking; he'd know better than that.

Wes pulled up his canteen and sipped a little water. He was dry after the long night ride from Eden City, but he hadn't allowed his companions to water themselves and the animals at Tonto Seep. He had been the first of them to reach the area and had met each of them as they approached the seep to turn them aside into the dry hills. He had been cursed aplenty, he knew, but not to his face. Ojo del Muerto Springs was ten miles to the east, but Wes didn't intend to stop there for water either. It was too obvious to anyone tailing someone from Eden City into the Espantosas' westward approaches. Wes and his party would have to make their next water stop at Soldier Camp Mesa, *if* there was water there this late in the year. It was too early for the fall rains. If Soldier Camp Mesa didn't have water in its three-tiered *tinajas,* there were two alternatives; one was to backtrail to Ojo del Muerto, and the other was to send a man to Lonesome Springs far to the north and east. Lonesome Springs was one of the few pools of 'live' water within the great ramparts of the Espantosas, other than Ojo del Muerto. Wes himself would have waited several weeks before attempting to penetrate the Espantosas. By that time the fall rains would have filled the *tinajas* with plenty of water But Buck Coulter was in too great a hurry.

The eastern sky was lighter. The wind shifted a little with the coming of the dawn. Wes looked down toward the unseen seep. Something was there. He hadn't heard or seen anything, but he knew that something or somebody was there. He glanced over his shoulder. He could still see the pinpoint of light. Wes felt about until his hand touched an egg-sized stone. He flipped it high into the air over the reverse slope and was rewarded with a thudding sound and a muffled curse, but the cigarette was crushed out.

Metal struck stone between Wes and the seep. Something jingled faintly. It was still as dark as the inside of a boot down in the canyon. It was quiet again. They weren't Apaches. He would not have heard them. Apaches moved like wind-driven smoke, completely silent and almost unseen. The thought of them made Wes' skin crawl a little. 'Broncos' still haunted certain areas of the Espantosas, but they would not go within half a mile or more of Ojo del Muerto. They did not have the same taboo on Soldier Camp Mesa and Lonesome Springs. Wes sometimes thought they let the White-Eyes *think* they would not go near Ojo del Muerto. What better way to lure the hated White-Eyes into a trap? A hoof rang against stone like a cracked bell. It was a shod hoof, but that didn't mean anything. An Apache would ride with pride a mount he had stolen from a white man. If those were Apaches down there, and they were tailing Wes and his partners, they would have shod their mounts with rawhide boots. A horse whinnied sharply. Wes wondered if the animal had caught his scent. Changed my drawers and socks just yesterday, he thought wryly.

Something moved softly through the darkness. A high-crowned hat seemed to swim into view, rising from unplumbed depths of darkness. Wes grinned. The best rule in Apache country, when fighting Apaches, was: "Shoot 'em if they don't wear a hat." God help any hatless white man who prowled around. A spur clicked against a stone.

A man coughed in the darkness closer to the seep. The wind shifted. Wes wrinkled his nose. One of the horses had crapped. The pungent odor carried along the canyon. The man just below Wes was moving around too much. A deaf man might have heard him, thought Wes.

The voice startled Wes. "Kelly! Where the hell are you?" Someone cursed in Spanish. The voice came again, as though from a disembodied spirit. "There ain't no one around, Kelly," it said. *He* was no greaser!

"I ain't so sure," said the man just below Wes. "I don't like the smell of this place."

The other man laughed. "Luis' mare just dropped a pile, Kelly. That's all!"

Kelly came up the slope and looked about. The light was a mite better now. "I didn't mean that, Carl," he said. "Sometimes you act like a mare shit in your face. Can't hear, see, or smell anything else."

"Kelly!" rapped out another voice. "How does it look?"

Wes lay lower. That last voice was the voice of Luis Galeras. The Galeras Bunch was up early. Wes wet his dry lips. It wasn't likely they were after Wes and his partners. Luis Galeras wouldn't even tackle Buck and Wes as a pair. It was a lead pipe cinch that Luis hadn't come into the foothills of the Espantosas just to wreak vengeance, as the dime novelists would put it, on the man who had just killed three of his band. Luis was after other game.

"They could be ten miles from here by now," said Carl.

"The old man cannot move that fast," said Luis Galeras. "They must have water soon. If they did not get it here, they must have gone on to Ojo del Muerto. I know these mountains. It is the only other place to get water for thirty miles."

"I ain't so sure," said Kelly.

"I say they're ten miles from here," insisted Carl.

"You say shit!" snapped Kelly. "How come you lost sight of 'em an hour after they left Eden City? An old man and a filly, and they get away from you! Jesus! I thought you said you onct scouted Apaches! They'd have scalped your ass whilst you was lying in the bear grass looking for sight of 'em!"

Wes grinned. It was just about what he would have said. The grin faded as he thought of the Fairbairns. The old man must have headed for the Espantosas, despite all the warnings he had received. Let the old coot die in his boots trying to find his dream, but why let the girl die with him? She would die harder if the broncos got hold of her, and perhaps even harder if the Galeras Bunch caught her.

"They must be on the way to Ojo del Muerto," said Luis. "Carl, go back and get Gonzalo. Kelly and I will ride on. Tell them to move fast. There is no time to lose."

Kelly came higher up the slope. "What about Yardigan and Coulter, Luis?" he asked.

Luis did not speak for a moment. When he did, his voice was hard with stored up venom. "Their turn will come," he said. "First the old man and the girl, then the others."

Kelly spat. "Maybe they're with Fairbairn by now," he said. "Jesus God, Luis! If we walk into an ambush, there won't be one of us get out of it alive. Coulter fights like a damned Apache, and Yardigan is almost as bad, maybe even worse by now. You seen what he done back in Brogan's."

Again the pause. "I have not forgotten," said Luis.

Wes felt a chill creep over him at the tone of the Mexican's voice. He rested his hand on his Winchester.

"Coulter and Yardigan will not be with the old man," said Luis. "Each to his own in this hunt for the gold, Kelly. Let's move out, amigo!" They walked down the slope to their horses. Hoof clattered on the harsh earth. Luis and Kelly rode east along the canyon bottom, and ten minutes later two more horsemen rode swiftly after them—Carl and the huge, dim-witted Gonzalo Baca.

Wes rested his head on his crossed arms. God help the old man and Lucy if Galeras and his cutthroats caught them. Why did that damned fool of an old man have to come into the Espantosas at all? Why did he have to drag Lucy with him? The lure of the Lost Killdevil was far too much for his addled head. It was Lucy who would suffer in the long run.

Wes put on his hat and worked his way down the slope in the graying light. Luis Galeras didn't know beans about the Espantosas if he thought there was no water for thirty miles with the exception of Ojo del Muerto. Kelly had been uncertain about that and Kelly had been right, but Luis Galeras was the leader and he wanted to go to Ojo del Muerto. Wes gripped his Winchester tighter. Chihuahua! What an ambush he and Buck could have rigged up for Luis Galeras and his muchachos! Between the two of them they could likely wipe out the whole rat pack of them. Wes suddenly stopped in his stride. Supposing Luke Fairbairn knew about the three-tiered *tinajas* at Soldier Camp Mesa? Just supposing Wes and his partners ran into Luke and Lucy there? It would likely be just as dangerous as if they had run into Luis Galeras and his boys at Ojo del Muerte.

"What did you see, Wes?" asked Buck out of the darkness between huge boulders.

"Luis Galeras and his boys," said Wes. "Man named Kelly and another named Carl. Four of them altogether."

"Tailing us?" said Buck.

Wes hesitated. "Quién sabe?" he said.

"Who else would they be after?" said Curly.

"Who said they were after anybody?" said Wes.

Curly laughed. "They're always after somebody, that's why, eh, Anselmo?"

Anselmo nodded. "That is so."

"You ought to know," said Wes. "You ran with that wolf pack long enough."

"I was immature," murmured Anselmo. He rolled his eyes upward. "When I was a boy, I thought like a boy. Now that I am a man, I think like a man."

"Amen." said Curly.

Wes took a cigar from his shirt pocket and lighted it. He drew in the smoke with satisfaction. "Begod, I needed that," he said.

"Can the rest of us light up, boss?" said Curly.

"Sure," said Wes dryly. "You hardly stopped, anyway."

"I got a lump on my cabeza because of your gentle way of letting me know I should put out my light," said Curly sourly.

"Next time, by God," said Wes, "I hope I fracture your gawd-damned skull! I could smell it clear up on the ridge!"

"Where were they heading?" asked Buck quietly.

"Ojo del Muerto," said Wes. Something was irking Buck.

"They must have said more than that," said Buck.

"It was all I heard," said Wes.

"You've got hearing like an Apache," persisted Buck.

"That was all he heard," said Curly as he lighted up. "If Wes says that was all he heard, then that was all he heard."

"You sound like the gawd-damned parrot," said Anselmo.

It was light enough now for Wes to see Buck's lean face beneath the hat brim. For a moment or two Buck studied Wes. "All right," he said. "What, now? You're the guide, Wes."

"Soldier Camp Mesa," said Wes.

"Maybe there is water closer," said Anselmo.

"Then, go there, by God!" spat out Wes. He walked to his dun.

"What the hell is rilin' him?" said Curly.

Buck Coulter did not answer. He limped after Wes, an unlit cigar clenched between his teeth. Now and then he glanced up at the broad back and wide shoulders of Wes Yardigan. The man moved like a hunting cat through the tangle. Buck himself could not have done any better in the old days. There wasn't any doubt in Buck's mind that he had picked the right man as guide through the Espantosas, and in a fight to the finish he'd rather have Wes Yardigan at his side than any other man he had ever known. Yet . . . The thought died aborning. Wes had committed himself to the venture. Buck and the two others would see to it that he kept his commitment.

There could be no long halts that day. They would have to press on to reach the water at Soldier Camp Mesa by dusk. As the day progressed the sun lanced down into the brush-choked canyons and turned them into a living, baking hell that first took the starch out of a man and then began to enervate him until the first faint mutterings of doubt and fear gave way to a soul-shaking desperation. The heat dried the juices in a man. First it attacked the skin and the outer layers of flesh, and then the thirst got into a man's blood and finally, as the day lengthened and the sun held full and unchallenged sway, the thirst crept into a man's very bones.

Now and then Wes glanced back over his shoulder as he led the dun through the tangled mazes of Lost Canyon. The damned cleft in the very belly of the Espantosas had never been lost; it was the poor souls who ventured into it that became lost. It was Buck that concerned Wes. The man must be going through secret tortures that did not beset the others. Even Wes felt the tremblings of fatigue in his legs. There were easier ways to Soldier Camp Mesa but none as secret. It had been years since Wes had traveled this way, a frightened lad of fifteen, led by Eusebio Ochoa, with the pack of hunting Apaches not a mile behind them and gaining every minute. He should have had more faith in Eusebio. The Old Man of the Mountains. Wes grinned. Eusebio had indeed seemed to be hewn out of the very rock of the Espantosas and roughly shaped into the semblance of a man. It was the eyes of Eusebio Ochoa that stayed in Wes' memory. Eyes the color of shale, as though shaped from the mountain rock. Secretive, searching eyes, always searching, searching for something that other men could never know. Wes had once heard that some of the conquistadores of old had such eyes.

Wes held up an arm to halt the rest of them. He squatted in the hot shade, shaping a quirley. He could feel the itching sweat running down his back and sides, soaking through undershirt and shirt. His throat was brassy dry. He lighted the cigarette and watched the others plod toward him.

Buck glanced up at the towering, riven walls, hung with great masses of rock that seemed ready to break loose and plunge hundreds of feet down into the canyon. It seemed as though a loud echo would loosen them. "Jesus God," said Buck quietly. The very nature of the place kept a man's voice low. Buck eased himself onto a flat rock, extending his crippled leg in front of him.

"Are you all right, Buck?" Wes asked in genuine concern. "Maybe you should have stayed behind."

Buck stubbornly shook his head. "How much farther?"

"Couple of miles."

"Which means the rest of the afternoon at this rate," said Curly. "Anyone else ever come in here?"

"I have," said Wes. He shook his canteen. It was empty. Supposing the three-tiered *tinaja* was dry?

"So has someone else," said Anselmo. "Look up there."

Someone had scratched a message into the decomposing rock above them. "Three Star Hennessy," read Curly. "Good for man or beast."

"Look further to the right," said Wes. "Someone else came after him."

"Repent or be damned," read Curly. He laughed loudly, awakening the sleeping echoes. "You don't suppose some ol' jackleg preacher even came in here lookin' for converts?"

"Why not?" said Anselmo. "They're all over this territory these days, like cowshit in a pasture, as Wes says."

"Anselmo is developing a sense of humor," said Wes. He slanted his hat across his eyes. "Next thing you know he'll become honest, and then we'll lose the good ol' Anselmo we knew and loved so well."

75

Buck shot an amused glance at Wes. "You've changed, anyway, Wes," he said.

"Yeh," said Curly. "You should have seen him when we found him in the Lagarto, eh, Anselmo? What were you really lookin' for out there, Wes? Your immortal soul?"

Anselmo lighted a cigarette. "Perhaps he was not looking for anything. Is it possible he was hiding from something?"

Wes sat down and stretched out his legs. "I've got nothing on my conscience," he said. "Even Buck has to admit he hasn't got any Wanted posters up for me in his marshal's office."

Buck studied his cigar. "Ex-office," he said quietly. He looked at Wes. "They wouldn't give me time off to come out here. I quit. They didn't seem too sorry about it."

"They'll never get another one like you," said Curly.

Buck nodded. "There might be more truth in that than you suspect, Curly. Besides, Duke canned me as well."

"What about Sophie?" said Wes lazily.

The gray eyes flicked cuttingly at Wes. "You've got a great sense of humor, boy."

Curly felt the tension. "Forget it," he said. "We'll all be millionaires by this time next week."

Anselmo looked up at the towering walls of the canyon. "If we ever get back out of the Espantosas," he said gloomily.

"Can that crap, Anselmo," said Curly quickly.

Anselmo shook his head. "It is daylight now," he said. "The blessed sun does not let the evils of darkness rise. But when the sun is gone . . ." His voice trailed away.

Buck spat to one side. "The evils of darkness?" he said bitterly. "Myself, I like the darkness better than the light. Everything is better then. It softens the harshness. It makes all women look interesting. It conceals the evils men do."

"You sound like you been readin' books," said Curly. He shifted his chew and spat. "Crazy," he added. "Wes was readin' books out on the Lagarto. He says they are the best friends a man can have when he is alone." He grinned. "Me, I'll take a bottle of booze and a woman."

76

"There is only one good book," said Anselmo piously.

"Yeh," said Curly. "But when did you ever read it?"

Wes stood up and stretched. "I hate to break up this discussion on good books," he said. "But it's time to move on." He led the way on up the canyon. He could not help but think of Luke and Lucy Fairbairn, who would be deep in the Espantosas by now. They might need help, but Wes could not leave his three companions until he had led them to water. In fact, he damned well needed water himself, and there was only one way to get it now and that was to keep on to Soldier Camp Mesa. Once in a while doubt would try to worm into his mind, but he drove it out as he drove himself on, pace by pace, into the rocky bowels of the Espantosas.

He kept watching those towering, crumbling canyon walls. Someday all the old signs and symbols would be gone by deterioration of the rock, and even now some of them were hard to find. Then he saw what he had been looking for. A long line had been cut into the canyon wall, and at the end of it, like a balloon fastened to the end of a stick, was an oval-shaped marking. He knew Buck was close behind him and he knew that Buck had seen him look up at the wall. "Spanish gourd," said Wes over his shoulder. He stopped and pointed, waiting for the others to come up with them. "Shadow wilting," he added. "Only about this time of day during the summer and early fall the sun strikes it in such a way that it may be seen."

"That means water ahead, eh, Wes?" said Anselmo.

Wes nodded as he led the way. The Espantosas were full of such markings. Some of them were of Indian origin and some of Spanish and the later Mexican, to be followed by the Americans. Some markings were truthful and accurate, while others were false and could easily lead a man to his death, one way or another, in the mountains. Old Eusebio had been a veritable dictionary of such markings and their meanings and he had passed on this lore to the boy he had raised as his own son. It was all that Eusebio had left to give. Shortly after Wes had gone out onto the Lagarto, the old man had been murdered.

Dusk touched the mountains with a velvety shroud as Wes stopped for a breather at the base of a great mesa that dominated the northwestern part of the Espantosas. Its great, riven flanks flowed broken rock and harsh earth down into the many canyons that trended toward the foot of the towering mesa. One canyon looked quite like another.

"This the place?" asked Buck from behind Wes.

"This is it," said Wes.

"How do you know, boy?"

Wes pointed to a marking on a tip-tilted slab of rock. It was partially concealed by brush, but part of a square had been scribed on the smooth surface, and the square had been divided into six equal parts by wavy lines. "Water nearby," translated Wes.

"Yes," said Anselmo. "But *where,* amigo?"

Wes pointed up the talus slope at the base of the great mesa. Faintly seen in the thickening shadows was the U shape of a mule shoe carved into the rock face. "Mule shoe," said Wes. "Indicates the trail is up there."

"Or treasure!" cried Anselmo. "That much *I* know!"

Wes wiped the sweat from his face. "You might be right at that, Anselmo. Only the treasure we are interested in at the moment happens to be the water, and we need that a damned sight more than gold or silver."

"Keno," said Curly. "Jesus, what a country!"

Buck nodded. "Go on, then, Wes," he said. "I know you won't fail us."

"Don't be too sure," said Wes.

Wes worked his way through the tortuous tangle of shattered rock and thorny brush, higher and higher on the slope until at last he stood just below the sheer rock face of an abutment of the mesa. He waited for the others. There was a trail ascending the rock face, hardly discernible at a distance except as a wavering hair line. Wes jerked a thumb toward the trail. *"Más allá,"* he said. "Farther on."

Curly craned his neck. "My God," he said. "Up *there?*"

"You want water, don't you?" Wes said cruelly.

Wes led the dun up the trail. It was pocked with holes

several inches deep, worn by the hoofs of burros and horses of many decades past. He glanced back over his shoulder. "This is the trail they used to bring down the ore. Tons of it. The old ore-crushing arrastres are over there beyond the slope. Don't get excited, Curly. There's no gold left up here. At least any that you can find. Eusebio Ochoa worked here in the old days, or at least I *think* he did. He must have been a muchacho in those days, for no one has worked these diggings for many years. The mountain 'walked,' he told me, and the shafts and drifts were poorly timbered. The timbers snapped and buried everything, including many of the poor bastards who were working in the diggings. He told me that one can still hear them on quiet nights, when the moon is full. They cry so: *Tortillaaas ... tortillaas ... tortillaas. Aquaaa ... aquaaa ... aquaaa.*" Here he had imitated the dry, cracked voice of Eusebio Ochoa to perfection.

Anselmo whirled, dropping the cigarette he was making. "Mother of God!" he cried. "Whose voice was that?"

Wes looked curiously at him. "Mine," he said. "Why?"

Anselmo swallowed hard. "Nothing," he said hastily. "It is not good to hear one speak in the voice of the dead." He turned away and began to make another cigarette.

"Listen to him," jeered Curly thoughtlessly. "Hey, Anselmo! You think old Eusebio will haunt you?"

"Shut up, you fool!" rapped Buck.

Wes had already started up the steep trail. He did not want Anselmo to see his face. No man with a guilty conscience should see such a face until the time of retribution is at hand.

Halfway up the rock face the cliff had seemingly been scooped out by a great shovel where a great fall or slippage had occurred long ago. The hoofs of the animals clattered on loose rock.

"My God!" yelled Curly. "This is ore! Good ore! By God, it looks as though it might have high assay."

"Gangue," said Wes. "Just waste from the mines that were once up near the cliff top. When the mountain 'walked,' those mines were buried forever, and the loose waste flowed down here to block the old trail."

"Wes," said Buck in a strained voice. "How much farther, boy?"

Wes ground-reined his tired dun. "Wait here, Buck," he said. "This trail is dangerous even during daylight." He padded forward, feeling for the rock face with his right hand. His tongue was slightly swollen, and his throat had a brassy taste. His body seemed drained of excess moisture, and his head throbbed violently. There just *had* to be water in the *tinajas!* If they were dry, they'd have to strike out for Lonesome Springs, but they would have to keep moving for twenty-fours through the darkness and the dawn to make it, and even Wes didn't feel quite up to that effort.

He worked his way through tangled brush and loose rock, half expecting to hear the strident rattles and then feel the stunning blow of a striking diamondback. The damned mesa was full of them. What in God's name am I doing here? he thought. His questing hands struck a rock face and felt along it. It was a man-made wall! He prayed silently as he pulled himself up it and over the edge. His feet struck dry rock. He was in the lowest level of the three-tiered *tinajas*. Wes pulled himself up with bleeding hands onto the wall of the second *tinaja*. He lowered himself into it. It was dry, too. His heart skipped a beat.

"Wes? Wes?" yelled Curly. "You all right?" The voice seemed to come from very far off.

Wes scaled the last wall. A faint odor came to him. Something scuttled off into the darkness. Wes hung over the wall on his lean belly, feeling for a match. He scraped it on the rock and held it down toward the bottom of the *tinaja*. The faint, guttering light showed a greenish surface inches from his big, sunburned nose. He swept the scum and pinkish bladders back and thrust a dirty pair of cupped hands down into the water. The pool was at least three feet deep. He closed his eyes in prayer even as he raised the gamey water to his cracked and swollen lips.

SEVEN

The moonlight shone down into the great hollow beside the *tinajas*. There was a faint flickering of firelight against the seamed rock face that rose above the hollow. Curly Killigrew squatted beside the upper *tinaja*, patiently straining water through a soiled silk scarf into a pot. "Deer tea," he said in disgust. "You'd think them damn-fool deer would know better than to foul the only drinking water they got for miles."

"Always bitching," said Wes as he unrolled his cantle pack. "If you don't like this water, sonny, you know what you can do about it."

"You can boil it, Curly," said Buck.

"Tastes worse thataway," growled Curly.

Buck winked at Wes. "Always bitching, like you say, Wes."

Anselmo stirred the bacon in the blackened iron spider. "Grub pile," he said. "Sowbelly and Mexican strawberries. Wes, hook that bean pot out of the coals." Anselmo filled the tin plates with bacon while Wes ladled out the Mexican strawberries from the pot. The four men hunkered near the fire, their plates raised beneath their mouths, shoveling in the food as fast as they could. One by one they finished and placed their plates to the side, feeling for their tobacco as they did so.

Wes stood up. "I'm going to take a looksee atop the mesa," he said.

"Not alone," said Buck.

"I'll be all right," said Wes.

"That's not what I meant, Wes," responded Buck.

Wes poured tobacco along the paper he held in his left hand. "What did you mean?" he said.

"It's better that we work in pairs," said Buck.

Wes rolled the paper and ran the tip of his tongue along

81

the edge to shape the cylinder of tobacco. "How do we split this up?" asked Wes.

"You and Anselmo. Me and Curly. That should do for a starter. Agreed?"

Wes shrugged. "Why not me and Curly or you and me for a starter?" Wes asked as he lighted his cigarette.

"Because that's the way I want it," said Buck.

Wes eyed him. "What you're telling me, then, is that you give the orders around here, is that it?"

"That's the size of it, Wes."

Wes nodded. He walked to his dun and picked up the saddle blanket. He could feel the eyes of the trio on him.

"Where are you going?" asked Buck quietly.

"Out of these damned mountains and back to the Lagarto," said Wes over his shoulder. It suddenly seemed inordinately quiet. He turned slowly to look at his three companions. Their eyes were set upon him, and their heads were lowered a little.

"Maybe you haven't got the idea yet, boy," said Buck.

"I had the idea that we had a partnership," said Wes.

"We do," said Buck patiently. He smiled a little. "That means we have to work together, not as individuals. We just can't let one of us go running off to look around on his own."

"You've got the *derrotero*," said Wes.

"And you have the lore of it and the fine memory," said Anselmo.

"If you had any sense, you trusting bastards," said Wes, "you'd know that the *derrotero* doesn't even show this part of the mountains. It shows you have to work east from Cuchillo Peak."

Curly spat leisurely into the fire. "So why do you have to take a looksee atop the mesa?" he said sweetly.

"You can see for miles up there in the moonlight," answered Wes. "I'm the guide, or does one of you want to take over?" He yanked the saddle blanket from the dun's back. "All right! Two of you go on up there so's we can keep this businesslike. Number off, partners, and move out when you're ready!"

Buck rubbed his jaw and looked down into the fire. He

looked up at Wes with tilted head. "All right, boy," he said quietly. "Maybe we're all a little edgy after today. Happens to the best of us, eh Wes? Even you, boy." He smiled. "Admit it."

Wes waved a hand. "We've been friends too long to let something like this treasure hunt break it up, Buck."

"That's the idea, Wes!"

"Keno!" said Curly.

Wes led the dun up the steep, potholed trail to the mesa top. The mesa top was brightly lighted by the moon and it had almost a dreamlike quality about it. There was no wind, and the growths and rock outcroppings sharply etched their shadows on the light-colored ground. Wes did not remain to enjoy the view. He rode the dun toward the eastern face of the mesa, overlooking a deep gash of a canyon that lost itself somewhere to the northeast. More than once he looked back over his shoulder, but he was not being followed. His bluff had worked, aided by the utter weariness that filled the three of them. It would be easy enough to keep going. He had left nothing behind that he could not replace. Wes would not keep looking for the Lost Killdevil if he deserted them. He had given his word to Buck Coulter, at least to the Buck Coulter he had remembered. The man himself was now different, changed a great deal more than Wes Yardigan had changed. It seems that those who change think the change is in everyone else, for they have neither the understanding or the humbleness to realize that the real change is in themselves. That, they do not want to face.

Wes reined in at the edge of the mesa overlooking a three-hundred-foot sheer drop to the talus slope below. To his right, concealed by a broken mass of overhanging rock, was a faint trail. He pulled off his boots and replaced them with a pair of tough, thigh-length, thick-soled, button-toed Chiricahua desert moccasin, the *n'deh b'keh*. He led the dun down the trail. Stones fell from the edge and rattled faintly far below. Wes did not look over the edge or he might have lost his guts, in more than one sense. Cold sweat had thoroughly soaked his clothing before he reached the bottom. He rode the dun across the canyon bottom. Once he stopped and scanned the mesa rim with his field glasses, but there was no one there, at least anyone he could see. "I'm not going to steal your gawd-damned mine," he said bitterly.

He rode toward a V-shaped notch in a hump-backed ridge. Every now and again he would halt the dun and sit in the saddle to look and listen. There wasn't any living thing to be seen. Still . . . It was a feeling that dogged one in the Espantosas. Eusebio had always said that the mountains were living things. There was another thing he had said, again and again, as though trying to impress it forever on the plastic memory of Wes Yardigan. "Never forget, chico," he would say, "that the mountains never give anything freely to man. It is certain that they ask a price, but that price no man knows until sometimes it is too late to go back. The Indians say that that which is taken from the mountains must sometime, somehow, be returned to the mountains. I think that is true. Some Indians are very wise. They have been here longer than any white men, but the mountains themselves were here long, long before any Indians."

An hour after leaving the bottom of the mesa trail, he was close enough to Sangre Cuchillo Peak to see where the great riven sides had buried their feet deep beneath the talus slopes that flowed fanwise into the canyons that opened toward the towering peak. From Soldier Camp Mesa, by way of the trail that led up to the three-tiered *tinajas,* it was at least five times the distance that Wes had traveled from the eastern side of the great mesa. He grinned to himself. Few men would have risked coming that way. "Dumb luck," he said.

A faint wind had begun to rustle through the canyons. Wes took his rifle and field glasses and then picketed the dun in a box canyon. He moved through the tangled brush and shattered rock like a puff of wind-driven smoke, until at last he lay belly-flat on a great tip-tilted slab of rock that overhung the huge semicircular pocket at the bottom of the eastern side of Cuchillo peak, wherein lay the ever-flowing waters of Ojo del Muerto, the Eye of Death.

The wind shifted slightly, and he caught the faintest whiff of tobacco smoke. Wes inched his way across the huge slab of rock until at last he could catch the odor of the fresh water. Thirst raked at his throat. From somewhere inside the towering granitic pillar seeped the clear, fresh water that filled the three pools of the springs to overflowing. Wes had once sounded those pools, finding bottom at six to ten feet in the first two pools, but in the third one, much farther down the slope, beneath a crumbling rock face that had partially filled the pool, he had not been able to find bottom at all. There must be thousands of gallons of water stored in the three pools. Wes forced the thought from his mind. "Deer tea," he said softly. "Oh, my God!"

A man coughed softly within the thick, velvety shadows that concealed the first pool. Wes rubbed his tired eyes. Was the old man that big a damned fool to camp at Ojo del Muerto? On the other hand, had Luis Galeras and his boys found the old man and Lucy there? Wes' skin crawled at the thought.

Wes hated the place. In the old days when he and Eusebio had passed by that way, they would water up and get the hell out of there. Wes heard a cough again. He picked up a stone and flipped it high into the air and was rewarded with a faint splash down at the pool.

"What the hell was that, Kelly?" a man said clearly.

"Shut up, you stupid bastard!" snapped Kelly.

Wes now knew where two of them were.

"I heard something," insisted the first speaker. It was the man Wes knew only as Carl.

"Keep quiet!" hissed Kelly. "You want to scare off the old man and the filly?"

Wes felt relief pour through him.

"You sure they're comin' here?" said Carl.

"I ain't sure of anything except I'll break your gawdamned jaw if you don't shut up!"

"They got to come here," said Carl. "It's the only water for miles and miles."

"For the love of God!" called out Luis Galeras. "Keep quiet!"

Ojo del Muerto reverted to its usual silent darkness. Wes backed down the slab and padded off toward the trail to the west. How had they missed Luke and Lucy? Maybe

85

the old man had gotten to the springs first, watered up, then had taken off into the maze of canyons east of the springs.

Wes left the trail as he reached a point half a mile west of the springs. There was a position there where he could see the trail both ways without being seen himself. The moon was bright on the light-colored rock. No one could pass on that trail without being seen from above it. Wes sat down, resting his rifle against a boulder. Where the hell was that addled old man?

Something double-clicked behind Wes. His blood seemed to fill with reddish ice crystals, and the hair stood up at the back of his neck. He raised a hand: "You touch that rifle," a cracked and familiar voice said just behind Wes, "and I'll blow off your gawd-damned thick head!"

"I was only going to scratch, Luke," said Wes.

"Then you itch, mister!"

"You touch off a gun up here," said Wes, "and those coyotes down at the springs will be breathing fire on your tail, mister."

Luke cackled. "Them? They're near as stupid as you are!"

"Gracias," said Wes dryly.

"Turn around! Keep them hands up!"

Wes raised his hands and turned to look into the muzzle of a heavy Sharps rifle. The muzzle looked as big as a mine drift. The old man's washed-out blue eyes had intermingled thoughts in them. Determination for one and madness for another.

Luke cackled again. "You young fellas," he jeered. "You think you know so much and you don't know nothing! Stand still! I'd have a .45/90 slug in your guts before you cleared leather!"

"You've got only one shot in that cannon," said Wes.

"Like to try?" challenged the old man.

"Put down that rifle, Grandpa," said Lucy from the shadows. "Wes means us no harm."

"You think your way, gal, and I'll think mine."

"You're out of your cabeza, Luke," said Wes.

"Nothing wrong with me!" snapped Luke.

Wes lowered his hands. "No," he said. "Not a damned

86

thing! You get that girl out of here and go back to Eden City and get a job for a change, if they'll hire a locoed old jackass like you!"

Luke shook his head. He lowered the rifle, but the muzzle still covered Wes. "You got no respect for my white hairs," he said sadly. "What's the world comin' to?"

"You won't be around long enough to find out if you don't pull foot out of here," said Wes. He took out the makings and began to make a cigarette. "There's four of them down at the springs, Luke. What chance do you have? I'm not too sure about Buck, Curly, and Anselmo, either."

"Why not? You're in with 'em, ain't you?"

Wes shrugged as he lighted the cigarette and hunkered down in the shelter of the huge boulder.

"Don't lie! That was a great act you put on in Brogan's Stable," said the old man. "You didn't fool me none!"

"Act?" said Wes feebly. He looked at Lucy. "Three men get killed, and he thought it was an *act*." He looked up at Luke. "I don't know what information you have on the Lost Killdevil. Maybe it's the missing part of the *derrotero*. I don't know, but I know this: the Galeras Bunch think you have it, and so does Buck Coulter. None of them would hesitate a minute to wring it out of your scrawny old hide."

"Maybe they ain't sure I have it," said Luke. "If I do have it," he added hastily.

Wes studied him. "Don't lie to me, you old goat," he said.

"Buck Coulter used to be my friend," said Luke.

Lucy came out of the shadows. "He used to be everybody's friend," she said.

"Lucy," said Wes. "Get your grandfather out of these mountains. He isn't going to find the Lost Killdevil. All he'll find is his own death."

"I'm staying!" snapped Luke.

"And you?" Wes asked the girl.

"I won't leave him," she said.

Wes shrugged. He crushed out his cigarette and picked

up his rifle. "Well," he said quietly. "I can do you one favor, anyway."

"We need no favors from the likes of you," said Luke.

Wes glanced at the girl. "Lovable old man, isn't he?" He walked down the slope and then looked back. Something seemed to stab at his heart as he looked at her. The moonlight was full on her face, and the wind stirred her hair.

"Throw in with us, Wes," said the old man. "With your help I can find the Lost Killdevil. Half a share is better than what you'll get from them coyotes you're running with, if you get anything at all."

Wes shook his head.

"Maybe I got an almost sure way of finding the mine."

"Maybe you have," said Wes. "I gave Buck Coulter my word I would help him."

"What did he give you?" said Luke.

Wes shrugged. "Once he gave me my life," he said. He turned on a heel and walked silently down the long slope to the trail.

"Damned fool," said Luke.

"I'm not so sure," said Lucy. "He's loyal at least."

Luke bit off a chew and rapidly worked it into juicy pliability, his beard waggling up and down. "Loyalty my foot," he said. "He's got gold fever. It gets them all in the end."

"Like you, Grandpa?" she quietly asked.

He turned to look searchingly at her. "You want to go back, girl?"

She smiled wearily. "No, Grandpa. I'm with you to the end."

He waggled his head. "You're a better man, for a woman, than them coyotes down there."

"Gracias," she said dryly. "Let's go now."

"Wait," he said. "We ought to hear some fireworks in a couple of minutes. A hurrahing. That's one thing Yardigan is good at. Maybe the only thing, eh, granddaughter?"

She sat down on a rock and rested her right elbow in

the cup of her left hand, supporting her chin on her closed right hand. "You're always right, Grandpa," she said.

He nodded his head, then looked closely at her. "Mind your own business, Lucy," he said waspishly.

A horse whinnied from the deep shadows as Wes lay in a rock hollow. He thrust forward his rifle. He flipped a stone down toward the unseen pool. It splashed. A man cursed softly. A shadowy figure drifted across an open area. It turned and looked up toward Wes, the face white and unnatural-looking in the moonlight. In the darkness beyond him Wes could see a pinpoint of light alternately growing and fading away, where someone was smoking. A horse whinnied again and came slowly into view, followed by a man in a steeple hat. Three of them were enough for a starter, thought Wes. He touched off the heavy rifle. The crashing discharge echoed and reechoed down several canyons. The cigarette light vanished. The man in the open sprinted for cover. Wes fired again. The slug ricocheted off the hard ground and screamed eerily into space. The man following the horse had turned to run. Wes fired swiftly. The man shrieked in pain and dived for cover.

Wes leaned forward. Boots thudded in the shadows. A man yelled from beyond the first pool. A horse whinnied in terror. Wes thrust forward the rifle and emptied the magazine of the last nine rounds as fast as he could fire. The crashing discharges and booming echoes almost deafened him. He rolled over and over down the rock slope and plunged into the brush, running silently on moccasined feet as he reloaded the hot rifle. As he darted to one side into the clinging brush, heading for his dun, he thought he heard a faint, cackling cry of malicious laughter up on the northern flank of Sangre Cuchillo Peak, but he wasn't sure. One could never be quite sure of anything in that haunted place.

EIGHT

Four well-armed men certainly had little to fear at Ojo del Muerto in broad daylight, but even so there was a vague uneasiness about the place. It had been two days since Wes Yardigan had hurrahed the Galeras Bunch at the springs. He had said nothing to Buck and the others when he had returned to the camp after midnight, when the moon was long gone. Buck and Curly had been sound asleep, and Anselmo sat with his back against a boulder, huddled in his serape, with his rifle across his thighs, sleeping as soundly as the two men he was supposed to have been guarding. Wes could have cut all of their throats in a matter of minutes.

There seemed to be no signs of Wes' shooting up the springs. Beyond the springs there was a pocket of softer earth washed down from the slopes above the springs, and it was in this pocket that the dead of many years had been buried. No one really knew how many bodies had been buried in that unhallowed makeshift cemetery. A few crude markers sagged from the vertical, but rain and wind had long ago erased the names of those who had been so identified.

Wes looked up from where he was studying the two pieces of *derrotero*. He eyed the low mounds and the sunken places of the graves. "Who killed them, and how well did they die?" he said.

Buck shifted his bad leg. "Who says they were all killed?"

"You think a man would choose this place to die a *natural* death, Buck?" Wes shook his head.

"You think a man chooses his place of death?"

"Animals do, if they aren't killed," said Wes.

"Man is not an animal, boy."

The sun glinted from the brass trim of Curly's rifle. He was standing guard quite near the place where Wes had fired from when he had rousted the Galeras Bunch from the springs. "Thinking animals, anyway," said Wes.

Buck smiled and shook his head. "You were out on the Lagarto too long, boy."

Wes made a cigarette. He glanced sideways at Buck. "Like the old prophets who went into the wilderness to grapple with their souls and fight temptation, eh, Buck?"

Buck laughed. "You were the one that said it, not me!" He looked curiously at Wes. "By the way, did you ever find your soul out there?"

Wes lighted the cigarette. He looked down into the clear waters of the first pool, watching the tiny, darting shadows of fishes. "No," he admitted. "Few men do, I suppose."

"You'll find it here in the Espantosas," Buck said confidently. "With gold from Killdevil a man can find his soul or buy it and anything else his soul desires."

Wes studied the *derrotero*. "We haven't found it yet, Buck."

"You've been looking at that chart a helluva long time without saying anything. Are you hinting that we won't find Killdevil?"

Wes blew a smoke ring and watched it drift out over the pool. "It's been lost a helluva long time, Buck."

Buck tossed a pebble into the pool and watched it sink to the clear bottom, stampeding the fish on the way. "We need the missing piece of *derrotero*, is that it?"

"It would help. There's something else that might be more valuable than that. A *conocimiento*, or waybill. With that, we might not even need the third piece of *derrotero*."

"Look, Wes," said Buck impatiently. "We haven't got the third piece, or the *conocimiento*, or whatever the hell it is! Now, you get started with what we have! Comprende?"

Wes nodded. He rolled the two pieces of *derrotero* together and scrambled nimbly up the broken rock face that overhung the three pools. He reached the top, a slanted area of naked rock, backed by yet another wall that rose perhaps fifty feet higher, overhung with a thatch of brush. There weren't any signs to be seen, and he hadn't expected any, but he knew there must be some means of guiding the searcher to the next sign. There had to be! Anyone who ever searched for the Lost Killdevil knew that. Eusebio Ochoa had known that, but he had never found it.

The rock faces were badly decomposed. Any signs that had been cut into them would have vanished long ago, and yet the Spaniards or Mexicans who had worked the Killdevil must have known that that would happen. Wes lighted another cigarette. He could see Anselmo far below him on the eastern slope below the springs. The sun glinted from his coin silver hat ornamentation. Wes padded about on his moccasined feet, scanning the rock face. He reached the area where the decomposed rock and loose earth had flowed down a V-shaped notch in the rock face to partially fill the third and last pool. Wes pressed himself flat against the rock face and looked out across the wide, heat-shimmering canyon to the east of Sangre Cuchillo Peak. Nothing . . .

He could see Buck limping back and forth, looking up at Wes. Wes placed the *derrotero* on the ground and studied it. There was something he had seen when Curly and Anselmo had first shown him the one piece of *derrotero* out on the Lagarto. He had not been sure at the time what it was. He studied the unusual symbol. It was somewhat oval-shaped, with one end rounded and the other almost pointed. He bent closer to the symbol. There were faint flecks of paint still fringing the oval. To the right of it, partially effaced by the worn and wrinkled edge of the chart, were some printed letters. "Sta," he said. He rubbed his jaw. "*Esta*? It is? Christ! That doesn't mean anything to me." He gently rubbed the hide with a wet finger and saw faint traces of two other letters before the letters *sta*. "Vista!" he said. He narrowed his eyes. He hunkered back on his heels and ran the various possible meanings of the word through his mind. "Sight, vision, view, landscape . . . Look, glance . . ." Wes rubbed his bristly jaw. He looked up across the great canyon. He looked down at the chart. He wet his finger and rubbed the curious oval-shaped symbol. "Sonofabitch!" he said quietly. "It's an eye! An eye, with *vista* printed next to it! Eyesight. Eyevision. Eyeview. *Eyeview!* That must be it!" He got to his feet and looked about him. A crumbling ledge spanned the rock and earthflow that fanned out to reach the third pool. Wes worked his way across it toward the rock formation that overhung a sheer drop of about seventy-five feet to the talus slope below. Bits of rock pattered on the slope as he crossed to the formation, and as he reached it a great piece of the ledge broke loose and plunged down into the third pool, creating a minor tidal wave that washed over the rim of the pool and flooded out into the brush and trees.

Sweat ran down his body as he clung to the formation. Right in front of him was a hole in the rock. A tenseness came over him. The hole looked natural, yet there was something quite different about it. He leaned closer. "By God," he said softly. "Drill tool marks!" He took off his hat and pressed his face against the rock, sighting through the hole. Across the shimmering heat waves that arose from the canyon he saw a great hump-backed ridge that slanted transversely into great folds of rock formed in some cataclysmic orogenesis of thousands of years past. Wes strained his eyes. There must be something over there. The hole slanted upward in line with great rock folds at the end of the ridge. He uncased his battered field glasses and placed them to his eyes, hanging onto the rock with his free hand. Sweat misted the eyepieces. He moved the glasses a little. Then he saw something. "Chihuahua!" he said hoarsely. He closed his aching eyes to rest them for a moment, then looked again. This time he was quite sure. A great triangle had been cut into the naked rock, although here and there parts of it were gapped where rock had broken or scaled off from the cliff face. But the tip of the triangle had not been disturbed, and extending from the tip was a great, curved line that pointed to a direction to the right of the triangle, the southeast.

"Wes!" yelled Buck. "Gawd-dammit!"

Wes slung the glasses around his neck and took a bearing on the triangle, memorizing distinguishing landmarks. He eased himself backward, then slid down on the steep talus slope, digging in his heels, riding to the bottom of it just above the spring in a swift rushing of gravel and earth. He stepped aside at the very lip of the water and jumped onto a ledge that was still damp from the overflow caused by falling rock. He worked his way around the edge of the dark waters of the pool, so different from the clear depths of the first and second pools. In time falling rock and sliding earth would eventually fill up the third pool.

Buck waited for him at the edge of the second pool. Even before Wes could speak, Buck reached inside Wes' shirt and withdrew the two rolled-up pieces of *derrotero*. "Help yourself," said Wes dryly.

"What did you see?" asked Buck in a taut voice.

Wes pointed across the canyon. "That ridge. Almost where it meets those humped rock formations. Above the end of the ridge. A great triangle with a curved line on top of it pointing to the right. Look through the glasses." He handed the glasses to Buck. Buck studied the rock. "Yes," he said at last. "I see it. What does it mean?"

Wes helped himself to Buck's cigar case. He bit off the end of a long nine and spat it out. "Follow the curved line to our right. To the southeast."

Buck lowered the glasses. "Is that all?" he said.

Wes lighted the cigar. "It's a lead, Buck. We might have missed it altogether."

Buck nodded. "We'll go on, then."

Wes looked up at Curly and whistled sharply three times. Curly came scrambling down the rocks. Wes could hear Anselmo calling to the horses and the burro. In a little while the Mexican brought the animals to where the saddles and the aparejo of the burro had been placed. While Wes and Anselmo saddled the horses Curly and Buck were in deep conversation as they filled the canteens and the two small water kegs.

Anselmo looked at Buck and Curly. "What is it they talk so secretively about, eh, amigo?"

"It isn't the weather," said Wes.

The one eye settled on Wes and the wandering eye joined it for a moment. "It is the wish of Buck that we two work together," he said.

"He has the great sense of humor," said Wes.

"I would not betray you. Would it not be best if we made a deal?"

"Such as?"

Anselmo wet his lips. "To back each other against them if they try to pull the fast one on us."

"What the hell is bothering you?" said Wes. He leaned against his dun and relighted his cigar.

Anselmo looked quickly about. "I am afraid," he said. "We are going into the stony heart of these accursed Espantosas. I feel that there is a fifth rider with us. One we cannot see, but he is there all the same. I speak of Death!"

"Bullshit," said Wes.

"But there is something evil about this place. You admit this?"

Wes shrugged. "You've got too much imagination," he said.

Anselmo leaned closer. "There is blood on the rocks over there." He pointed into the thickest part of the growths that fringed the pools. "It was not spilt there too long ago."

"Some cougar got a deer maybe," said Wes.

"I doubt that," said the Mexican. He wiped the sweat from his dark face. "Look," he added. He felt inside his shirt and withdrew a piece of crumpled and dirty white cloth. He unfolded it. "See! Blood spots, amigo! This has not been here long!"

Wes tightened the cinch on his dun. "Here come the others," he said over his shoulder. "Get rid of that."

Buck limped up. "How long will it take?" he asked.

"The going is hard," said Wes. "What do you think, Anselmo?"

Anselmo shrugged. "Three or perhaps four hours. No more."

"Water?" said Buck.

"Lonesome Springs, eh, Wes? There is grazing there as well," said the Mexican.

"Is that on the way?" asked Buck.

Wes blew a smoke ring. "That depends on the next sign we find, if we find another one. The triangle is on the *derrotero*. The next sign, according to the *derrotero*, should be southeast of the triangle, as the triangle indicates, but I am not sure whether or not the next sign on the *derrotero* was destroyed by the tear between the two pieces of hide. It will take some guesswork."

"What's the problem?" said Curly. "It's bound to be up the next canyon or so."

Wes looked at him. "Christ," he said. "You're a great help! There must be at least a dozen canyons up that way, and every one of them as bad or worse as the one we followed to get to Soldier Camp Mesa. Eh, Anselmo?"

"That is so," said the Mexican. "The mine will not come up and hit you in the eye, Curly."

"Let's get moving, then," said Buck. "Andele!"

Curly swung up into his saddle. "By the way," he said. "Look at this." He held out a hand in which there was a spent brass cartridge case. ".44/40 and fresh-fired, from the looks of it. There was eight or nine more up where I was standing guard. You can still smell the burnt powder in 'em."

Anselmo's eyes swiveled slightly toward Wes and then away. Maybe the Mexican was onto something, thought Wes.

"You carry a .44/40, Wes," said Buck.

"So do Curly and Anselmo," said Wes easily.

"They didn't leave Soldier Camp Mesa that night we camped there," said Buck.

"Who did?" said Wes. He swung up into his saddle.

"You sayin' you didn't?" challenged Curly.

"It's one helluva big mesa," said Wes dryly.

"Maybe you got some explainin' to do," said Curly.

Wes leaned a little toward him. "And maybe I don't," he said. "We came in here to hunt down the Lost Killdevil and so far we've got a good lead. You aimin' to stand around here all day? You coming along, or do I go alone?" He touched the dun with his heels and rode down the tree-shaded slope out into the burning sunlight.

"What the hell is rilin' him?" said Curly.

Buck mounted his sorrel and thrust his cane into the saddle sheath alongside his Winchester. "Nothing of importance," he said. "Trouble with you is you don't realize you're dealing with one of the squarest men who ever walked these damned mountains."

As the last hoofbeats echoed from the base of Sangre

Cuchillo Peak and then died away Ojo del Muerto Springs returned to the peace and quiet that was its natural existence. The water rippled in the dry wind that crept up from the sun-drenched canyon. Now and then a cottonwood leaf would drift slowly downward to alight gently on the water, rising and falling on the tiny wind ripples until it drifted beneath the rock ledge that overhung the edge of the pool. A climbing uta lizard scurried across the rock face and dived into a deep cleft. Somewhere in the deep shadows at the base of the towering peak a mourning dove softly called: "Coo-ah, coo, coo, coo . . . Coo-ah, coo, coo, coo . . ." The faint and haunting sound drifted off to die away in the great canyon. There was peace and quiet again at Ojo del Muerto Springs. When Man the quick killer was not around, Ojo del Muerto Springs was a quiet and lovely place.

NINE

"Parate!" barked Anselmo. He thrust up an arm and then led his horse behind a great slab of tilted rock that stood close to the base of the cliff that towered above them. The Mexican stood looking to the west as the others led their mounts into concealment. "Look!" he said over his shoulder. "There it is again!"

A shard of reflected light glanced through the shimmering air above the canyon. There was no sign of living creatures in that great, heat-reeking trough of rock. "Field glasses," said Buck quietly. "The question is: did he see us?"

"The question to me is: how long has he been watching us?" said Curly. "He could have been watching us at the springs."

The swift shard of reflected light flicked out again. Whoever was scanning the canyon was almighty careless about shading the lens against the sun. That wasn't like Luke Fairbairn.

They waited a long time in the hot shade behind the huge slab of rock, smoking and hunkering on their heels, while Anselmo watched the far canyon wall. "Nothing," he said at last. "The way along the base of this cliff and up onto the ridge is not visible to them over there."

"Lead out, then," said Buck. He watched the Mexican lead his lathered horse into the thicket beyond the slab of rock. "You don't suppose that was someone signaling to him, do you?" he quietly asked.

"He was the one who seen it," said Curly.

"Doesn't mean a damned thing," said Buck. "The fact that he was the first one to see it would just as well throw suspicion off him, wouldn't it?"

"Never thought of it that way," said Curly. "Who'd be signaling to him, anyways?"

"The Galeras pack," said Buck. "He was an amigo of theirs for years." He looked at Wes. "You suppose those bastards are around here somewhere?"

"If they smell gold, they'll be around," said Wes.

"I'll give them a smell of powdersmoke and blood," said Buck. He took the reins of his sorrel and followed Anselmo.

Curly shaped a cigarette and thrust it into his mouth. "Sometimes he gives me the creeps," he said.

"Anselmo?"

Curly shook his head. "Buck," he said. He lighted the cigarette. "Come on, before he thinks we're plotting against him." He led his horse out onto the trail.

Anselmo was working his way through the tangle like a seamstress threading a needle. The sun was slanting low to the west, but the heat of it was still thick and cloying in the canyon. They could not see the great, carved triangle on the cliff face that towered above them, but it didn't matter. There was only one way to go—along the rock face toward the many smaller canyons that debouched into the greater one they were in.

The sun was gone when they made their camp in the first canyon, south of the great triangle marking. There were others beyond this first canyon, every one of them a hell of fallen rock, tangled, thorn-tipped brush and thick-bodied diamondbacks. Anselmo made the smokeless fire

98

in a deep hollow set into the southern wall of the canyon and once the food was cooked, he allowed the fire to die down into a thick bed of embers. The four of them ate in silence broken only by the gnawing of teeth against hard biscuit or the liquid slurping of the hot, strong coffee.

Wes sat silent after he had eaten, watching the changing patterns in the embers and listening to the dry moaning of the wind as it blew down the canyon.

"There will be a good moon tonight," said Buck.

"It won't keep me from sleeping," said Curly.

"Yes it will," said Buck. "Once the moon is up, you backtrack on foot and keep watch at the mouth of this canyon."

"Why?" said Curly.

"You saw those reflections," said Buck. He lighted a cigar with a burning twig.

"I can ride back," said Curly.

"Your horse needs the rest more than you do," said Buck.

Curly opened and then closed his mouth. When Buck Coulter talked like that, one *listened*. It was very dark now, and the faint light of the glowing embers shone on the faces of the four of them.

"Can you work by moonlight, Wes?" said Buck.

"If it isn't 'shadow writing,'" said Wes. "We'll need the sun for that. They'd have to be on the north wall to catch the sunlight. It's possible but hardly likely that the moon would have the same effect."

"Have you ever been in this canyon before?" asked Buck.

"No," said Wes. "At least I don't think so."

"That's a great help," said Curly sarcastically. He was taking out his spite on Wes.

Wes looked at him. "So far you've contributed exactly nothing but sheer stupidity to this expedition," said Wes.

Curly opened and closed his mouth. He saw the same look in Wes' eyes that he had seen in Buck's eyes.

Anselmo filled his coffee cup. "I have been in here before," he said.

"Whyn't you say so, then?" snapped Curly. He wasn't much afraid of Anselmo.

"Because I was not sure," said the Mexican. "Perhaps the mountains change and move around when one is not in them. Quién sabe?"

"Listen to him!" jeered Curly.

"He might be right at that," said Wes.

Buck smashed a hard fist down upon his thigh. "Just make sure of yourselves," he warned. "Don't tell me about mountains moving about."

The wind whispered through the canyon and then died away. It was very quiet. Something howled faintly far up the canyon. Anselmo's head snapped up. "Satan's Horns!" he cried out. "What was that?" Sweat greased his dark face.

"Coyote," said Curly.

"Coyotes do not usually come in here," said the Mexican.

"Wolf, then," said Curly with a sly grin. "What the hell is the difference?"

The haunting cry came again, but it seemed to be closer. Anselmo shifted nervously. "There have not been wolves in these accursed mountains for many years."

Curly lighted a cigarette. "Well, maybe it ain't exactly the kind of wolf *you* was thinkin' about."

Anselmo stared at him. "What do you mean?"

Curly waved a hand. "One of them was-wolves."

"Werewolf," said Wes. He shook his head. "Jesus God, Curly, haven't you ever read a book?"

"The almanac," Curly admitted, "but I never learned a gawd-damned thing from it."

"That figures," said Wes dryly.

"It is *not* a wolf," insisted Anselmo.

Curly spat carelessly to one side. "Apache, then?" he said.

Anselmo shook his head. "That is no human voice," he said in a low voice. "I can tell!" He got up on his knees and crawled to a boulder, over which he peered with fearful eyes. Buck got to his feet and limped over behind the cringing Mexican. "Damn you, Anselmo!" he spat out. "Cut out this superstitious talk! You won't be worth a

100

damn to any of us this way!" Anselmo leaped fearfully to one side when he heard that whiplash voice, as though he had been struck from behind. He slipped on the slick rock, and his left hand was planted fully in the embers of the fire. He shrieked like a wounded animal. He rolled over on the ground, clasping his burned hand to his chest.

Wes leaped to his feet. "Let me see that hand, amigo," he said.

"I'll take care of him," said Buck. He drew out his sheath knife.

Wes turned his head. Buck walked over to Anselmo and gripped him by the right arm, lifting him easily to his feet. "Let me see that damned hand," he said. "Wes! Get that tin box from my left saddlebag." Buck forced open Anselmo's left hand. "Hold his hand open, Curly. Now!" Curly held the trembling hand open, and Buck nodded. He kicked some dry brushwood onto the fire and in the renewed light of it he patiently picked out the ashes and the bits of charred wood from the burned flesh. He smeared the hand with ointment from the tin box and expertly bandaged the wound.

Wes uncorked a brandy bottle and handed it to Anselmo. Anselmo drank deeply and nodded his head. "Esta bueno, amigo," he said weakly. He sat down with his back against a boulder and cradled his hand in his lap.

Buck wiped clean his knife blade and then sheathed the heavy, razor-edged weapon. "You'll be all right, amigo," he said kindly. "I didn't mean to startle you, Anselmo, but a blind man is better on a treasure hunt like this than one who has lost his guts. Comprende?"

Anselmo nodded. "Yo comprendo," he said quietly.

The first traces of moonlight began to show in the eastern sky. Curly picked up his rifle and a canteen, nodded to the others, and then walked out into the still-shadowed canyon.

Buck unscrewed the top of his cane and shook out the two rolled pieces of *derrotero*. He placed them on a flat rock and then smoothed them out. Wes added fuel to the crackling fire and stood beside Buck, looking down at the aged chart. "See here," said Wes. "There is the great triangle we saw." He placed a nicotine-stained finger on it. It was right at the junction of the two pieces of hide, and the wrinkled edges made it difficult to decipher any symbols in that area. "Trouble is," added Wes thoughtfully, "a symbol must have been destroyed, the symbol that would have indicated *which* canyon to enter."

"Our best bet, then, boy," said Buck, "is to work up this canyon in the moonlight. If we fail here, we can try the next canyon and so on."

Wes shook his head. "Helluva big canyon country and probably waterless as well, Buck."

"What about Lonesome Springs?"

"They are northeast of us. We'd be working away from them, toward the southeast and farther away every day."

A match snapped into flame in the shadows away from the fire. The flicker of light revealed the dark face of Anselmo as he held the match to the tip of a cigarette. "Somewhere east of us," he said, "there is, or was, a *tinaja* of green water. There might be some water in it at this time of the year."

"We'll chance it, then!" said Buck.

Wes shook his head. "No, we won't. By God, Buck, if it *is* dry, we'll be signing our own death warrants."

Buck laughed. "Where's your gambler's blood, amigo?"

"I bled it all out on the Lagarto."

Buck hunkered back on his heels, rubbing his crippled leg. "So what do you suggest, Wes?" he asked.

Wes lighted a cigarette, never taking his eyes from the *derrotero*. Every time he saw it, he added a little more of it to his memory, filling in the *derrotero* he carried in his mind. He placed a finger where the upper left-hand portion of the *derrotero* was missing. "I calculate Lonesome Springs is right about here. We can hunt for symbols tonight and get some sleep after moonset. Tomorrow morning I can take the burro to Lonesome Springs for water and be back no later than the next morning."

Buck shook his head. "I need you to decipher this chart."

"Send Anselmo, then," said Wes.

"Alone?" said the Mexican.

Buck ignored Anselmo. "Curly can go," he said. He looked sideways at Wes with a slantways grin. "It was you yourself who said he had contributed nothing so far except sheer stupidity. I couldn't have worded it better myself." Buck stood up, rubbing his aching thigh. "By God! If we only had that third piece! I feel we're close! So damned close!"

Anselmo drew in on his cigarette. "It is said that treasure appears only when unsought, and then in the most unlikely places." He flipped the cigarette butt into the fire. "The moon rises."

They took their horses and rifles, some rope, a light spade, and their personal canteens. The heat still filled the trough of the canyon like a thick, woolly blanket, pressing down and keeping back the fresher, cooler night air that was beginning to rise up the canyon.

By the time they were halfway up the canyon, the moonlight had fully tipped the eastern heights and had begun to flow down into the canyon like a film of mercury. They waited until the floor of the deep trough was fully lighted by the moon. The canyon curved gently to the right, trending toward heights of folded rock and broken-topped pillars as naked of growths as sword blades. Three pairs of eyes eagerly scanned the canyon walls. They moved slowly on.

"Goddammit to hell!" barked Buck after half an hour of silence.

"Nothing on the walls," said Wes. "That isn't to say there couldn't be markers elsewhere. They don't jump out and hit you in the eye, that's for certain sure."

"That third piece of *derrotero* grates in my craw," said Buck.

"God never made it easy to find a fortune," said Anselmo piously.

"Amen," said Wes.

Buck glanced sideways at Wes with a sly grin. "Sometimes I feel that you don't have your heart in this hunt. Is gold of no value to you now, my desert philosopher?"

Wes shrugged. He scanned the towering walls. Buck

sometimes had a neat and uncanny way of reading Wes' mind.

"Gold is of value to all men," said Anselmo.

"Every man has a price, eh, Anselmo?" said Buck.

"I'm not so sure, Buck," said Wes. "It's the price you pay that makes me wonder about the value of the whole business."

Buck laughed. "You'll live to kick one helluva hole in your share," he said.

"If it is enough," said Wes. He lighted a cigarette.

Buck stared at Wes. "What do you mean by that?"

"We don't know how much gold is left in Killdevil," said Wes. "Maybe it's run dry, Buck, like last night's whiskey bottle, with all the joy and pleasure gone forever. Maybe it's just another hole in the ground, and God knows the Espantosas have plenty of those."

Anselmo shook his head. "Jesus Melgosa said he had left more *quinientos* of pure oro in the mine than he had ever taken from it."

Wes laughed. *"Quinientos?* Five hundred pounds of ore? Maybe he did leave it, but did he say how much it assayed?"

"Damn it, Wes!" snapped Buck. "Do you have to tear down everything?"

Wes eyed his friend. "Why do you have to build it up? You might have been taken by a myth, Buck. A pig in a poke. Just remember that we can ride out of these mountains as broke as we came into them. You'd better make that reservation."

Anselmo had wandered up the canyon, staring at the walls, then at the ground, like a questing hound.

Buck shook his head. "I can't make such a reservation, Wes." His voice broke a little. "I've got to find that mine! I have no alternative, Wes. Nothing!"

"Hola!" cried out Anselmo.

"He's found something!" said Buck eagerly. He snatched up his cane and limped after Anselmo.

Wes lighted another cigarette. He blew a smoke ring and watched Buck hobbling toward the Mexican. *"I've* got to find that mine," he had said. Not *we,* but *I.* The distinction cropped up in his speech all the time.

Anselmo stood on a tilted slab of rock, deeply sunk into the hard soil at one side where soil and detritus had been washed down from the slopes above it. Anselmo triumphantly pointed to a carved curlicue in the rock. "Hola," he said.

Wes took his light spade and carefully scraped away at the baked soil that covered the sunken end of the slab. He took out his sheath knife and picked out the soil that had filled in on the carving. Parts of it had been effaced, but there was enough of the carving left for him to identify it. It was an upside-down letter U with the ends curled over, almost touching the sides of the letter. "Ascending moon," he said. "It means look, or go higher."

"It's not on the *derrotero*," said Buck. "Maybe it was cut off when the hide was separated."

Wes looked along the canyon side above them. It still curved to the northeast. The talus slopes were fully lighted by the moon, but high above them was a great arched vault worn into the living rock. The interior of the vault was dark in shadows.

"Look there!" said Buck. "There's a great ledge along the front of that vault! Could that be the mine?"

"Loco place for it," said Wes, "but, then, gold is where you find it, like they say."

Anselmo started transversely up the slope. The man could move like a mountain goat. His horse kicked loose bits of rock that clattered down the talus slope, raising a thin film of acrid dust. Buck and Wes led their mounts after the Mexican. The sharp clattering of the hoofs and the falling rock echoed and reechoed from the great vault and rebounded from the far side of the canyon, until it sounded like a troop of cavalry trotting on pavement.

Anselmo was high above them when he stopped. "Before God!" he cried out in astonishment. "Look at that!" He pointed into the huge, towering vault. Buck and Wes reached the Mexican, and the clattering of the hoofs died away into silence. It was now very quiet. It was better so, for what they saw in wonder had existed throughout the lonely quietness of centuries. There was enough reflected moonlight to see within the vault, and it revealed a series of man-made structures that entirely filled the rear of the vault from one curved and overhanging end wall to the other, while over the structures the dome itself overhung the vault like a gigantic, protecting seashell. The structures rose three stories high in some places, while here and there crumbling towers rose yet another storey. Tiny windows and T-shaped doorways stood out in sharp shadow relief against the pale, grayish-white stone of the buildings. A low wall ran the length of the ledge in front of the cave dwellings, standing up at the very edge of the talus slope.

"By God," said Buck. "I've heard about them being in here, but I never knew anything as big as this existed."

Anselmo's face was a dark study of superstitious fear. He crossed himself. "This is not a good place," he said in uneven tones. "These *montezumas* are said to be haunted!"

Wes led his dun up the slope and then threw a long leg over the ledge. The dun scrambled over after him. Here and there on the uneven pavement of the terrace in front of the dwellings were squared holes from which protruded crude ladders. Wes pointed to them as Buck leaned on the wall from the outer side. "Kivas," said Wes. "The Pueblos still use them. Sort of a combination religious room, clubhouse, and secret society for the men." '

Buck nodded. He shoved back his hat. "The mine wouldn't be here, most likely."

"It's obvious," said Wes. "If the Spaniards or Mexicans had come in here, they wouldn't have left one rock upon another if they suspected *oro* or *plata* was in there."

"There is nothing in there," said Anselmo hastily from down the slope. He looked down at his feet at a rounded surface that protruded from the talus. "Look! Here is a large olla! It will do well for a water container."

"Be careful you don't break it," said Buck.

Anselmo got down on his hands and knees in the bright moonlight and carefully began to work away the loose rock from around the pot. Wes led the dun along the terrace, scanning the dwellings as he did so, wondering how many centuries had passed since the Ancient Ones, as the other Indians called them, had left them forever. He stopped at the far end of the terrace, where the wall had crumbled down onto the slope. He felt for the makings.

Anselmo screamed like a frightened woman. Wes whirled, raising his rifle. Anselmo was on his feet, staring at what he had uncovered when he had lifted the big pot. A grinning human skull stared back at him from the shallow hole the pot had covered. Anselmo ran down the slope, with loose rock clattering far below him and dust drifting in the light wind. His horse trotted after him.

Buck shook his head. "By God, Wes," he said. "He's lost all his guts." He looked at the skull. "Friend of yours?" he added.

Wes slid down the slope and picked up the pot. It was black-on-white work and beautifully done. He looked at the ancient skull. "Your need is greater than ours," he said dryly as he placed the pot over the skull.

Anselmo had vanished into a brush thicket far down the slope. A thin wraith of drifting dust marked his hasty passage. Wes grinned and then started to laugh, passing a hand over his eyes. "Did you ever see anything like that before, Buck?" he called out. He took his hand from his eyes and looked up at Buck and, as he did so, he thought he saw something move in one of the windows of the tallest of the crumbling towers. It was so startling that he thought he might have given himself away to Buck. He walked up the slope, trailing his rifle, watching the tower out of the corners of his eyes. Buck took a bottle out of one of his saddlebags and held it out toward Wes. Wes shook his head. Buck drank deeply, and as he tilted back his head Wes again saw something in the window. This time his sighting was more definite. "Jesus God," he said under his breath. He had seen a white beard, although the face of the man had been indistinguishable. It must be Luke Fairbairn. Oh, the old coot was slick enough, but he had let his beard betray him.

Buck wiped his mouth, corked the bottle, and slid it into the saddlebag. "Keno," he said. "Now I've got the strength to go on, boy." There was no indication that Buck had seen anything.

Wes waited for Buck. The man was limping badly. Old Luke had evidently been long gone from the Ojo del Muerto area by the time Wes and the others had reached the springs. In order to hide in the ancient dwellings he would have had to get into the canyon ahead of Wes and the others. If that was so, who had been watching them from the far side of the canyon that day? Wes slowly shaped a cigarette. He looked out of the corners of his eyes at the dwellings. She must be with the old man. He could almost feel her presence.

"What's bothering you, boy?" asked Buck as he limped up.

"Nothing," said Wes.

Buck glanced at Wes. "You think that loco Mexican has pulled foot on us?"

Wes grinned. "He could be back in Eden City by now at the rate he was moving."

The voice sounded farther up the canyon slope. "Hola! Hola! Hola!" cried Anselmo. "To me, amigos! Hola! Hola! Hola!"

"By God!" said Buck. "He's found something! That took the fear out of him! Come on! Vamanos!" He struggled along the slope as fast as he could go, dragging at his sorrel's reins.

Wes shook his head. "Gold fever," he said quietly. "It took the fear out of Anselmo and the pain out of Buck. I wonder what it can do for me? He glanced at the cave-dwellings. They looked as though no human foot had disturbed their ancient dust in centuries. He followed Buck along the moonlit slope.

TEN

Anselmo was down on one knee, closely examining a small rock. He looked over his shoulder with a wild, exultant gleam in his good eye, while the other one wandered about aimlessly. "The *mulatress* does not sleep alone!" he said. He held out the rock to Wes.

"Well?" said Buck.

"Oxide of iron," said Wes. "Surface rock containing

oxide of iron. It's supposed to keep close to gold or silver. The Mexes say they always 'sleep' together."

"Superstition?" said Buck.

Wes tossed the rock up and down in his big hand. "I doubt if anyone knows more about mining lore than they do." He looked about. "This looks like anything but gold or silver country. Still . . ."

"Busque! Busque! Busque!" cried Anselmo. He was off again like a questing hound.

"He's a good one," said Wes. "You knew what you were doing when you picked him out. But, then, he did have another piece of the *derrotero,* didn't he?" Wes walked on after the Mexican. Buck looked thoughtfully after Wes. His eyes narrowed, as though he couldn't quite figure out what Wes had in mind.

There was plenty of time before the moon disappeared. The terrain had suffered agonies in some vast cataclysm of the past. Folds of rock had been forced up from beneath the surface, splitting and shattering the sedimentary rock that had formed the original surface on a level with the canyon floor, which was now far below the three men. There was almost a dreamy quality about the area. The heat of the day was gone, and a cool, dry breeze swept across it. It was pleasant enough to the eye, but always in the quick and perceptive mind of Wes Yardigan there lingered something that persisted in intermingling with his other thoughts. It was as though someone, or something, were watching him from a distance, but even if one were to turn quickly to see it, there was nothing there, almost as though it had anticipated the movement and had skipped swiftly out of sight. Wes had experienced this same feeling before, particularly out on the Lagarto Desierto, but there was a different quality to it in the Espantosas.

Anselmo had vanished into a maze of shattered rock that had flowed on the lower slopes from a naked dome of granitic rock. Again he sounded, like a belling hound, "Hola! Hola!"

Wes followed after the limping Buck. Now and then the man staggered in his haste as his weak leg gave way. Wes came up behind him and looked into a circular cove of rock, perhaps fifty feet across. Anselmo held up a curved piece of rusted metal. "The shoe of a mule! See! There are many of them! See! Another and another!"

"A good haul for the junkman," said Wes dryly.

"Why here?" said Buck. "Dammit, Wes! There are dozens of them!"

Wes took his light spade and worked his way through the tangled growths at the rear of the cove. A sunken patch of soil drew his attention. He drove the spade into it. It was softer than the surrounding ground. Wes turned over the spade and exposed a blackish, crumbling soil. He rubbed it between his fingers. "Charcoal," he said. He felt about in the loosened earth and withdrew a short length of rounded metal. He whistled softly. "Drill steel! They had a forge here. Sort of an outdoor blacksmith's shop. They shod their animals here and treated their drill steel to harden it."

"God knows it!" crowed Anselmo.

Buck shoved back his hat and looked about. "How close is it?" he said. "That's the big question."

"They'd need water hereabouts," said Wes.

"But there is no water here," said Anselmo.

"There could have been," said Wes. He made a cigarette and tossed the makings to the Mexican. "Which reminds me, Buck, we'll have to have water by tomorrow night at the latest."

"Curly can go for it," said Buck. "Damned nuisance!"

Wes grinned. "Going for the water or Curly?"

Buck bit off the end of a cigar. "Both," he said.

Wes cupped a light in his hand for Buck. "Take it easy" he said with a smile. "The Killdevil has been lost for about forty years. It can stay lost a little while longer."

"You think this is it?" said Buck. He waved a hand at the cove and then the surrounding terrain.

"Quién sabe?" said Wes.

Buck shook his head. "Curly contributes absolutely nothing," he said. It seemed to be a fixation with him.

Wes walked to the mouth of the rock cove. "Nothing but loyalty, Buck," he said over his shoulder.

Wes walked about, scanning the heights around them,

looking for a symbol, a pile of gangue, a trail, or anything that might suggest the presence of a mine. He shook his head, and as he did so something rolled beneath his left foot. He picked it up. It was a 'miner's spoon' of burnt soapstone, used for stirring quicksilver into other metals. "Anselmo!" he called out.

Anselmo trotted over to Wes and looked at the spoon. "Christ's Blood!" he yelled.

Buck came slowly toward them. Wes held up the spoon. "Maybe he used it for his chile beans," said Buck.

"No," said Anselmo, completely missing the joke. "It is the real thing!"

Wes shoved back his hat. It was a puzzler. There must be a mine close by, but this area was covered by the *derrotero*, and there was no indication on it of the mine's being the Lost Killdevil. By all Wes' calculations the symbols for the Killdevil should be on the missing piece of the chart. Yet there was almost indisputable evidence that some mine was in the very area where they now stood.

Anselmo was gone again. This time he came racing back with something in each hand. In the right hand was a rawhide guarache, or peon's sandal. In the left he held a peculiar corroded brass cartridge. "The sandal is hard with age," said Anselmo excitedly. "There are many of them over there hidden beneath a rock ledge. It was the custom in the old days to wear such sandals in the mines and cache them when the mine was not being worked."

"Burnside cartridge," said Buck. "See the banded middle, Wes?"

Wes nodded. "Jesus Melgosa carried a Burnside years ago. Burnsides were used as far back as the Fifties. Quite a few of them during the war. I've seen some of them out here not too long ago. That cartridge could have been lying out here thirty years or more."

"Look!" said Anselmo. "There is a sign! Like a sunflower! What does it mean?"

Wes looked at the symbol carved on the rock formations to his left. "Petroglyph," he said.

"Whatever the hell that is," said Buck.

Wes shrugged. "Indian sign," he said. He grinned. "Old

Eusebio once guided a professor through the Espantosas, searching for such petroglyphs. Eusebio couldn't get over the fact that the learned man was not interested in symbols for gold and silver but only in petroglyphs." As he turned to look again at the cartridge and sandal his eyes caught something high above them, almost under the lip of the cliff to the north of them. Time had worn much of it away, but there was no mistaking the shape of a bowie knife, cleverly carved to follow the natural configurations of the rock face. The knife symbol seemed to fade in and out of the vision, so cleverly had it been reproduced. Wes pointed to it.

"It points to the mine?" said Buck in a low voice.

"More likely to the next sign," said Wes.

"But it points back the way we came," said Buck.

Wes nodded. He took the *derrotero* from Buck's hands and placed it flat on the smooth ground at his feet. "Beats the hell out of me," he said. "There ain't no such animal on this chart." He looked up at the symbol again. "No question about the direction," he added.

Anselmo was rooting around beyond the area where they had found the mule shoes and the drill steel. His hat popped up out of the brush, followed by his dark sweating face. "Here is an arrastre!" he called out. "Here they crushed the ore!"

"By Christ," said Buck. "We're close! So damned close!"

Wes looked about. "There was a mine near here. No question about that."

A gunshot sounded in the canyon far below them. The flat echo bounced between the canyon walls and died away.

"Take a looksee, Anselmo!" called Buck. He limped to his sorrel and withdrew his rifle from its saddle scabbard.

The Mexican worked his way through the thick brush of the lower slopes. Wes faded away behind a boulder. Buck was already under cover. Minutes ticked past. A horse whinnied sharply, and then a burro brayed raucously. Two men appeared down the slope. One of them was

Anselmo, and the other one couldn't be anyone but Curly Killigrew, leading his horse and the heavily laden burro.

"What the hell is with him?" said Buck angrily.

"Likely he got lonely," said Wes. "Curly is a great one for augering, and you can't talk to yourself *all* the time."

Curly came sweating up, dragging at the reins. "Anselmo says you got some good leads," he said breathlessly.

"Who told you to leave your post?" said Buck coldly.

"Hellsfire!" said Curly. "Wasn't anyone but me and my fleas sitting around down there. I figured I'd save time and bother by bringing up the burro and the gear."

"What was that shooting about?" asked Wes.

Curly shoved back his hat and scratched his head. "Damned if I know what it was."

"You did the shooting," said Buck.

Curly bobbed his head. "By God, it was scary, I tell you! I was coming along under them ruins down there. The moonlight was right on 'em, makin' 'em look scary like. Well, they didn't bother ol' Curly none, I tell you, until I seen something."

"Such as?" said Buck.

Curly looked about himself, as though someone else might be listening. "I got a weird feelin' somebody was watchin' me from that old *montezuma*. All of a sudden I *did* see something! A white thing, moving out of sight in a window. I raises my rifle and lets drive but didn't hit nothing far's I could tell."

"Lousy shooting," said Wes.

Anselmo shook his head. "What he saw was not of the flesh, I tell you!"

"Bullshit!" said Buck. "You damned fool! That shot could have been heard for a mile or so because of the canyon echo. If anyone has been following us, they know for sure where we are now."

Curly flushed. He awkwardly waved a hand. "Well, I guess you're right, Buck. I just got excited."

"Scared, you mean!" rapped out Buck.

Curly looked away, like a child that has been severely reprimanded. He looked at Wes for sympathy but didn't see any in Wes' eyes. Anselmo had vanished again.

"We'll need water," said Buck.

"I'll go in the morning," said Curly.

Buck shook his head. "You'll go tonight. You hear me? You've got enough moonlight to get a good start. You can sleep until dawn and make the springs during the morning. I want you back here no later than dusk tomorrow. Comprende?"

Curly nodded dumbly. He watched Buck limp off to find Anselmo. "What's rilin' him?" he said.

"Tired," said Wes. "Leg must be giving him hell."

Curly looked sideways at Wes. "How close are we?"

"Can't tell," said Wes. "It's close, whatever it is."

"Killdevil?"

Wes shrugged. "It can't be, according to the *derrotero*." Together they unloaded the burro. They emptied the kegs into a hollow in the rock for the animals to drink and filled every container they had with water from the extra canteens. They lashed the kegs onto the burro's packsaddle and slung the empty canteens over them. Curly mounted his claybank and looked down at Wes. "You look after my interests, eh, Wes?"

"Why not?" said Wes. He grinned. "I doubt if I'll have much to look after, Curly."

"You got any hard feelings toward me?"

"No," said Wes.

Curly smiled. "I didn't want to leave without clearing that up."

"You'll be back, amigo."

Curly nodded. He touched the claybank with his heels. "I used to have a damned good job fixin' windmills onct," he said quietly. "Not much pay, but you sure could see a lot of nice country whilst you was workin' up there." He rode off, followed by the patient, trotting burro.

"Watch your back, amigo!" called out Wes. "You keep eyes in the back of your head all the time. You hear?"

Curly looked back with a faint smile. "I hear you," he said. "Wes, if you find gold, you put on a damned good drunk for me!"

Wes watched him ride out of sight. The man sounded as though he weren't coming back. Something was bothering the smiling one—something deep, something he could not express.

Wes walked back to the rock cove where they had found the mule shoes and drill steel. He started a fire to make coffee. Now and then he looked uneasily up at the heights. He didn't know why, but something always drew his attention to them. He was used to being alone; he had liked it in the Lagarto, but here it was different. It was always different in the Espantosas. Again and again the thought came to him of Curly Killigrew riding on into the gathering darkness with the sound of the hooves echoing from the narrowing canyon walls, and if he stopped to listen, the utter silence of the Espantosas would move right in on him.

Wes let the firewood die down to a thick bed of embers. The moonlight was almost gone, and there was no sight or sound of Buck and Anselmo, almost as though they had been swallowed by the night. "Few men die natural deaths in the Espantosas," the mind voice said clearly. It startled Wes. He had not heard it since he had left the Lagarto.

"Coffee ready?" a voice said out of the darkness behind Wes.

Wes threw himself sideways and clawed for a draw, whipping out the heavy Colt, thumb fanning back the spur hammer and stabbing the six-gun in the direction of the voice. There was a fraction of an instant when he would have fired and he would not have missed. Slowly he lowered the Colt, letting down the hammer to half cock. Cold sweat broke out on his body.

"For God's sake, Wes?" said Buck. "What's riding your back, boy?"

Wes sheathed the Colt after revolving the cylinder to let the hammer rest on an empty chamber. "Nothing. Where's Anselmo?"

"He'll be along," said Buck. He limped to a rock and seated himself, resting his back against the rock wall behind him. He leaned his cane on one side of him and his rifle on the other. "Coffee perking?" he asked.

Wes nodded. He looked slantwise at Buck. "What are you holding back, Buck?"

Buck grinned. "Can't fool you, eh, boy?"

115

They heard Anselmo outside of the rock cove. He came into the faint light of the embers, his face aglow with excitement. He held something in his hands. He extended it to Wes. It was a piece of age-stiffened hide fastened between two roughly shaped stretchers. The handles were smooth with usage.

"A *parihuela!*" said Wes. "Where did you find it?"

"For the carrying of the ore!" said Anselmo. "There is a slit canyon over there. It is not the kind of place into which one would stroll with his sweetheart, *but,* for the finding of a lost mine, yes! I feel we are close, amigo!"

The wind had shifted a little with the coming of the darkness. Wes filled the coffee cups. He placed the pot back into the embers. Somewhere up the canyon the wind sounded like the faint howling of an animal. Anselmo stopped his cup halfway to his mouth. "You hear that?" he gasped.

"I heard nothing," said Wes.

Buck went along with the joke. "Quiet as a graveyard," he said. He opened his cigar case. "Just imagination, Anselmo."

The howling sound came again, closer this time.

Cold sweat dewed Anselmo's face. "There are no coyotes or wolves in these mountains," he said slowly. *"That,* one knows.

It was very quiet. Buck and Wes watched Anselmo out of the corners of their eyes. Anselmo got unsteadily to his feet and passed a trembling hand across his mouth. An aura of green fear seemed to come sourly from his coldly sweating body.

"Sit down, amigo," said Buck easily. "Have some brandy with your coffee. It's only the wind, Anselmo."

Anselmo walked uncertainly toward the mouth of the cove. He stared out into the windy darkness.

"Do not be afraid, amigo," said Wes. "We will protect you." He winked at Buck.

Anselmo turned slowly. His eyes were wide. "It was not for myself that I am afraid," he said quietly. "It is for Curly." He crossed himself. "May he be protected by Our Lady Mother."

Somehow the joke was gone from the situation.

ELEVEN

Once during the night Wes awoke out of a deep, dreamless sleep. The fire had almost died out, leaving a thick bed of ashes through which now and then a tiny red eye of fire peeped out and then closed. Wes raised his head. Anselmo lay belly-flat on his blanket with his serape covering him. Buck lay flat on his back with his hat slanted across his face and his boots standing beside the foot of his blankets. Wes arose on one elbow and looked about. The wind was shifting and dying away. The dawn was not far off. Wes closed his eyes and fell asleep.

The dawn wind blew into the cove and whirled up the ashes of the dead fire, furring the blankets of the sleeping men. Wes coughed as the ashes blew across his face. He sat up and pulled on his extra shirt against the chill of the dawn. He felt about for his moccasins and pulled them on. Buck coughed in his sleep. Wes piled dry wood atop the ashes and lighted a fire. While the crackling wood worked down into a bed of embers he filled the coffee pot. Curly would miss his coffee this morning. He added more firewood and then sliced the bacon into the spider. The false dawn was tinting the eastern sky when Anselmo awoke, shivering in the cold. Wes shaped a cigarette and thrust it into the Mexican's mouth, cupping a match about the tip of it. "Coffee on the way," he said.

"How about me, boy?" said Buck.

"I don't know where you hide your cigars," said Wes.

Buck sat up and grinned. "I'd let you have more of them if you knew how to appreciate them, Wes. I'll swear you'd smoke dried goat manure and wouldn't know the difference."

"Does it look like a good day?" asked Anselmo.

Wes squatted near the fire, stirring the bacon. "You mean for finding a lost gold mine, or just the plain,

117

old-fashioned kind of a good day when you're broke and dumb happy?"

Anselmo sniffed the wind. "There might be rain," he said. "The heat has gone."

"The sun isn't up yet," said Buck. "It's too early in the season for rain."

"All the same," said Anselmo wisely. "I know."

They ate the meal and gathered together their gear. Wes watered the horses with the last of the water. He came back to the others. "Digging will be dry work," he said.

"Curly will be back this afternoon," said Buck.

"He better be," said Wes.

Wes whistled softly as Anselmo led the way into the slit canyon. The entrance to it was hardly more than thirty feet wide, a great V-shaped slit in the rock. The farther in Wes got, the less he liked it. High on the naked rock walls were ledges and clefts hung with the gray fragments of long, dried brush and driftwood, mute evidence of what a flash flood could do in there, a frothing, churning, insensate horror that would sweep everything before it, flora and fauna both, while great rocks would grind along the hard bottom with a dull roaring that would melt the guts in a man.

The canyon widened with terraces of rock and earth on either hand. The three men walked slowly, scanning the walls for symbols or any indication of a hidden mine. It was Anselmo who saw the first sign, not far from where he had found the *parihuela*. "Look!" he said, pointing high on the wall. It was an inverted U with lines extending at right angles to each side of the letter, and within the letter itself there were many dots pecked into the rock surface. "Closed mine or tunnel," said Wes.

"Look on the other side of the canyon," said Buck.

Wes turned. A numeral 5 had been cut into the rock, and the tail of the numeral had been curved to the right, carrying across the rounded lower part, while beyond the numeral were some short horizontal lines. Wes counted them. There were forty of them. "The tail of the numeral indicates the direction. Each horizontal line indicates the length of one vara, or thirty-three and a third inches."

"By God!" said Buck. "We've got it!"

118

Wes shrugged. "I'm not sure about the combination of the numeral 5 and the forty lines. It might mean to add five varas to the total or it might mean to multiply the number of varas by five. Your guess is as good as mine."

Anselmo took a length of light line and carefully knotted it at intervals of about thirty-three inches. Wes took one end of the line, and Anselmo walked ahead with the other, stopped when he reached the length of the extended line, and then Wes walked to Anselmo and passed him. The measurement of forty varas was reached where the canyon had widened with broad terraces on each side. The Mexican scrambled up onto the high right-hand terrace. He paced back and forth. "The flood water does not come this high," he said.

"You hope," said Wes.

Anselmo jumped up and down. "Listen!" he cried.

Wes climbed up beside him. He could hear Buck's cane tap-tapping on the hard earth of the canyon bottom. Anselmo jumped up and down again. This time Wes caught the faintest of hollow sounds. "Maybe an underground stream channel," said Wes. "Try again."

Anselmo clambered onto a rock and poised himself. He jumped heavily. The ground broke beneath his booted feet. He screamed as he broke through into a hole. Wes threw himself flat and caught the Mexican by the rolled collar of his charro jacket a second before he shot out of sight. The sudden halting of Anselmo's body almost dislocated Wes' shoulder. Anselmo screamed again and again, and the sound was eerily hollow. Buck clambered up beside Wes and gripped him by the legs. Slowly and carefully Wes lowered his left arm into the hole. Dirt and stones pattered down onto the coldly sweating face of Anselmo. Wes drew the man up, feeling the edge crumbling beneath him. "Pull back!" Wes yelled at Buck. Buck dragged on Wes' legs as Wes struggled with the squirming, screaming Anselmo. Finally Wes released the hold of his left hand and slapped the Mexican sharply across the face. "God damn you!" he yelled. "Don't fight me!" Anselmo instantly quieted down. Inch by inch Wes worked him out of the hole and at last got to his knees and dragged the man out flat on the ground. Anselmo lay there with sweat streaming from his face, and his head and hands shook as though he had the ague.

Wes' body trembled with the strain he had been under. "Another second," he said quietly, "and Anselmo would have explored the bottom of that hole the hard way."

Buck was looking up on the canyon wall as though nothing had happened. He pointed upward. "Look," he said quietly. Half effaced by time and weathering was a carving. Some of it was still obvious. "A sunburst," said Buck. He knew what it meant. The meaning was always the same. *Minerals or treasure close by.*

While Anselmo recovered, Wes cut away the loose edges of the hole until he could lie belly-flat with some safety, although he took the precaution of a lifeline tied to a nearby boulder. Buck had fitted together the folding lantern and had filled the oil reservoir. He attached a light line to the bail and then lighted the lantern. Wes lowered it slowly down the hole. The opening widened, angling back on either side. The lantern swung back and forth, and in the flickering light Wes could see pick and spade marks on either side. He lowered the lantern still farther until it hung thirty feet below him. "Chimney mine," said Wes over his shoulder. "Funnel-shaped. Typical of the old Spanish and Mexican mines." He slowly pulled up the lantern.

Anselmo had recovered. He held out a small pinkish rock to Wes. "Rose quartz," he said. Their eyes met knowingly over the rock.

Wes crawled back from the hole and lighted a cigarette. Something was puzzling him. Something wasn't quite right.

"Do you think this is it?" said Buck.

Wes looked up at him. "No, I don't," he said. "But look at it this way, Buck—this is a mine. There is, or was, gold in it. That's all we know so far."

"How can you tell it isn't the Killdevil?" Buck asked tensely.

Anselmo wiped the sweat from his face. "Wes is right. We've found a mine, all right. I myself do not think it is

120

Killdevil. There is one way to find out if this mine will pay off, and that is to go down into it."

None of them spoke again as coils of rope were straightened out and tested. Anselmo skillfully tied one length to another, while Wes attached a wooden seat to the end. Buck attached a double loop of rope to a boulder and fastened a block to it. It was very quiet in the narrow canyon. The sunlight was growing brighter, and some of its heat worked into the canyon, but it did not promise to be a hot day. Anselmo had said rain was due. The Mexican had a nose and an eye for weather. He was seldom wrong in his predictions.

"Who goes?" said Wes. He glanced at Anselmo, but the Mexican acted as though he had not heard Wes.

"My leg," said Buck. "It would stiffen in that seat. I'd be useless down there."

"That leaves me and you, amigo," said Wes to Anselmo.

The Mexican did not look at Wes. He glanced at Buck. He had evidently begun to trust Wes more than he did Buck. Wes could almost read Anselmo's racing mind. If Anselmo went down into the hole and found gold, could he be sure he'd be hauled up again to the surface? If he did not find the gold, it would be an easy matter to get rid of him by cutting the line, and his piece of the *derrotero* would be safe in the pocket of Buck Coulter.

Wes had no great desire to go down into the mine. Some Mexicans called them *estufas,* or stoves, with good reason, for they could be as hot as the belly of a cast-iron stove. He made a loop for the handle of his light spade and slung it over his shoulder. He filled his pockets with extra matches, several candles, and a small reserve can of lantern oil.

"Ready?" said Buck.

"Keno," said Wes. He got into the seat and sat at the edge of the hole. Anselmo gripped one of Wes' wrists to ease him down into the hole.

"Vaya con Dios, amigo," he said. Wes looked closely at the Mexican's face. Fear was still etched upon it. Under ordinary circumstances Anselmo was as brave as any

121

man, but the Espantosas and what had happened to him there was just too much for him and his superstitions.

Wes looked at Buck. "One jerk on the line means stop. Two means lower away. Three means to haul me up. Four means trouble."

Buck grinned as he had used to grin in the old days. "What's the matter, boy?" he said. "You worried, too?"

"I notice it's ol' Wes going down into this *estufa*. That's all I mean, Buck." Wes lowered the lantern down into the hole. "Lower away, Buck." Anselmo eased Wes down into the hole until the line was taut with his weight; then he crawled back to help Buck.

Wes swung gently back and forth as he was lowered. A dry and musty smell hung about him. He reached a cribbing area. The juniper wood logs used in the cribbing were just as sound as the day they had been placed in the mine. The sides of the mine were now vertical. He jerked the line once and as the motion was halted he lowered the lantern to the full extent of the light line. It swung back and forth, casting eerie shadows upon the dusty cribbing.

"Anything wrong, amigo?" yelled Anselmo.

Wes looked up to see the Mexican's hat and head silhouetted against the daylight. "Okay!" yelled Wes.

"Okay! Okay! Okay!" throatily echoed the mine.

"A lot you know about it, you dumb bastard," said Wes.

Wes fashioned a cigarette as he swung there. He lighted it and dropped the burning match down the shaft. It flicked out far, far below. Wes jerked the line twice and down he went once again. The black mouth of a drift surprised him, although he should have expected it by now. He jerked the line and as he swung toward the drift mouth he saw the remains of a ladder fastened to one side of the drift. He caught at it and swung himself into the drift, then slid from the seat and tied it to one of the ladder uprights.

Wes held up the lantern. The drift seemed sound enough, well propped with juniper wood. He walked in twenty feet and came to a blank rock face scarred with tool marks. There was no indication that gold or silver

122

had ever been removed from the drift. He walked slowly back and tested the ladder. It seemed sound. He gripped the lowering line and jerked it twice, then held the line as he worked down the ladder to the next drift.

A cool and invisible hand of air touched his hot face as he looked into the drift. Somewhere at the far end of it there must be an opening to the outside air. He walked cautiously forward, testing the drift floor with his spade. It was a typical drift of the Old Ones who had mined those areas. It gophered in, following the vein, instead of the way Americans mined by shafting and drifting, then cross-drifting to pick up the vein. Dust arose about his face. He kicked aside a broken and rusted pick of un-doubted Mexican origin. Here and there he passed rawhide *parihuelas,* stiffened with age and furred with dust. He rustled his feet through a pile of dried sotol stalks, which were used instead of blasting powder in the old days. A hole was drilled, then the green stalk was inserted and heated so that the sap steam burst and broke away bits of rock.

He reached a narrow-mouthed cross drift and held his lantern into it. Just within the reach of the light he saw a hole in the drift floor through which protruded a notched cottonwood log worn smooth by the contact of bare and sandaled feet. He tested the 'chicken ladder' and found it solid enough. He let himself down into the lower drift. The end of it was filled with fallen earth and rock through which protruded broken pit props. A pile of *zurróns,* or hide ore bags, lay to one side. Wes kicked at them and stepped backward to avoid the thin and acrid dust, and as he did so his left foot stepped off into nothingness. He went down on his right knee and felt it slip from the edge. The lantern fell and went out, but as it did so Wes snatched desperately at the pile of *zurróns,* and his clutching hands struck something bricklike and solid. His legs kicked at the air, and far below him he heard the pattering of bits of rock falling into the black depths. Crawling fear rode in on the sable wings of the utter darkness. The bricklike objects began to slide, but in a last effort he managed to pull himself back up onto the drift floor. Cold sweat burst out on his trembling body. He pressed his face against the *zurróns,* trying to control his shaking body and to drive the green fear from his mind.

Slowly he felt for a match and a candle. He lighted the candle and a foot in front of his bit nose he saw the bricklike objects that had saved him from falling to his death. "Oro," he said at last, and then full recognition came to him. "Oro! Oro! Oro!" He sat up and placed a hand on one of the massy objects. He hefted it. There were others half hidden beneath the dusty *zurróns.* "By God," he said in a low voice. "We've struck it!" He grinned foolishly. There was no one to hear him. Wes Yardigan was alone in the very bowels of the Espantosas with a fortune in his dirty hands.

Suddenly he raised his head to listen. There was nothing. He looked about before his attention was drawn by the lodestone of the gold that lay in front of him. The ore had been molded into crude, bricklike chunks called iguanas or lizards, by the old Mexican miners. He turned one over. It was marked with the embossed letter V and a Christian cross. "Jesuits, I'll bet," he said quietly. "They were a long way from home." He scraped at the metal with his sheath-knife point and raised a fine, wirelike spiral of pure gold. He counted the iguanas. There were ten of them, weighing about three pounds apiece. Wes did some mental calculation. At the going rate there was about seven thousand dollars' worth of gold lying in front of him. Not much of a haul for four men and a predatory woman, but Wes was satisfied. His share would be enough for a part payment on that spread in the Chiricahuas. He found the lantern and relighted it. The thought of Lucy Fairbairn flicked through his mind. Wes narrowed his eyes. Was there some correlation between the ranch in the Chiricahuas and Lucy Fairbairn? It was almost as though she had spoken to him.

Wes covered every inch of the drift, looking for more iguanas. He himself was satisfied, but he knew Buck never would be. The way Buck talked, seven thousand dollars would be a spit in the bucket for his needs. Wes kicked the pile of iguanas. They were the sum total of the gold, at least in that part of the mine.

There was a soft rushing sound in the darkness behind

him. He whipped out his Colt, thumbed back the hammer and whirled about, thrusting the Colt toward the sound. There was nothing there except a new flow of earth on the drift floor. It was an eerie, disquieting place. The earth was uneasy. Wes remembered all too well the story Eusebio Ochoa had told him about the old diggings at Soldier Camp Mesa, and of how the mountain had 'walked,' snapping the pit props and burying many men alive.

Wes picked up a *zurrón* and tested it. The hide was stiff but still sound. He loaded the iguanas into it and hauled it up the ladder. It took him ten minutes to search the other cross drifts. There was no sign of gold in them, but now and then he noticed the little piles of loose earth that had worked between the aged pit props to form little playas on the flooring of the drifts. Once he heard the faint cracking sound of a pit prop. Wes lugged the *zurrón* to the mouth of the drift. He fastened the lantern to the light line and lowered it, hanging out as far as he could to see if there were any more drifts below him. But there were none. He could just make out the bottom of the shaft, filled with fallen rock, pieces of broken cribbing, and earth. Even as he looked a piece of rock fell from the shaft and clattered down into the bottom of the shaft. Wes would be playing out his luck if he stayed in the mine much longer.

"Wes! Wes! Wes!" yelled Buck down the shaft.

"I'm okay, Buck!" he yelled. "We've struck it, Buck!" He leaned out and could faintly see a head silhouetted against the daylight. The head moved back. Wes fastened the *zurrón* to the seat, and then a cold, disquieting thought came to him. Once the iguanas were up on the surface and counted, maybe Buck and Anselmo would decide that Wes could fend for himself down in that damnable pit. He couldn't be hauled up first because there would be no way to bring the gold up after him, or at least *he* wasn't going to figure out a way.

"Wes! Wes!" yelled Buck. "Send up the loot! You can come up on the next trip after that!"

"These drifts are collapsing!" yelled Wes.

"You can wait a little longer!" yelled Buck. "We can just about haul you up!"

"You'll *have* to make it!" yelled Wes. He could hear Buck cursing and Anselmo's excited voice in the background. The Mexican would likely fill his baggy drawers with the impetus of his excitement. Wes got into the seat and gripped the line, jerking three times as hard as he could. He swung out into the shaft with the lantern swaying crazily back and forth, casting crazy shadows on the sides of the shaft. A moment passed, and then the slow ascent began. He passed the last of the cribbing. The hole was about fifteen feet above him. He crashed into the side of the shaft and damned near fell out of the seat. As he worked himself back into it he heard a muttered exclamation above him. A stone hit him on the shoulder. "For Christ's sake!" he yelled in mingled fear and rage.

The light was suddenly blocked out from above him. A scream echoed down the shaft, and the line jerked as something heavy struck it. A body smashed against Wes, almost driving him from the seat. Instinctively he grabbed out and caught a wrist. The contorted face of Anselmo looked up at him. "For the love of God!" Anselmo screamed in terror. "Do not let go!"

Wes began to feel himself slipping from the narrow board. He reached up and twisted his left hand into the ropes above his head. He began to tilt sideways. Anselmo's left wrist slipped a little through Wes' hand. The grease of sweat prevented a firm grip. Wes slipped a little lower. Anselmo thrashed back and forth. His foot kicked the still-burning lantern from the light line, and it fell swiftly to crash far below, splattering burning oil on the shattered pit props and broken cribbing at the bottom of the pit. Slow, lazy flames flickered up.

Wes felt himself going. His right hand slipped a little further. "Pull up! Pull up!" he screamed up the shaft.

Anselmo clutched at the gold-laden *zurrón*. The lashing knots tightened. His body struck the side of the shaft with a sickening sound. The seat began to twirl around as the line became twisted. Wes was now almost horizontal, his moccasined feet striking the side of the shaft, and his head almost touching the other side. Matches fell from his pocket and struck the sweating face of the Mexican. "Mother of God!" yelled Anselmo. "Do not let go!"

Wes' hand slipped. He could feel the bandage on Anselmo's hand. Now he tilted slowly, head downward, and he could see past the screaming Mexican to where the fire was gathering strength far below, lighting up the sides of the deep shaft. Smoke began to drift upward. Anselmo coughed harshly.

"Pull! Pull! Pull!" yelled Wes. The line did not move upward, but now it began to twirl back the other way. Wes' head struck the hard side of the shaft with cruel force, and his hand slipped again. His right hand was numbing from the hold he had.

With a supreme effort Anselmo pulled himself up, so that his contorted face was a foot away from Wes' face. "Before God," he said hoarsely. "I did not mean to kill the old man, but he fought like a madman. I did not mean to kill him!" His voice rose in pitch as he slipped again. Wes tried to tighten his hold on the dangling Mexican. The line that held the *zurrón* parted, but Anselmo did not let go of it. The added thirty pounds was too much. Wes' hand slipped onto the bandage, which slipped on the Mexican's badly burned hand and then came loose. With an ear-piercing scream Anselmo fell headfirst down the smoky shaft, still clutching the *zurrón*. His body struck heavily, scattering the burning wood. The flames leaped up angrily. Wes could see the Mexican's dark face in the bright light. The eyes were wide open in a sightless stare. Scattered about Anselmo were the golden iguanas.

The line tautened, and then Wes began to slowly rise, spinning about like a teetotum. At last he got his left arm up through the hole. He pulled himself up, straining, in deadly fear that he would fall to his death as Anselmo had done. He pushed his right hand through the hole and felt about until he found the line. He gripped the line and pulled himself from the hole with smoke swirling about him. Wes coughed and coughed as he bellied along the hard ground and then fell flat. He looked at his right hand. It still clutched the filthy, blood-stained bandage.

Wes raised his head and looked up into the taut face of Buck Coulter. "Where's the gold?" said Buck. "That poor bastard," he added.

Wes dropped his head. He passed a hand across his burning eyes. "Look down the shaft," he said.

Buck dropped flat on his belly and worked himself back to the shaft opening. He peered over the edge, coughing in the thick smoke. Wes heard a faint thudding sound far below in the shaft.

"Is that all of it?" asked Buck over his shoulder.

"Count it," said Wes dryly.

"Don't get funny!" snapped Buck.

Wes bellied alongside the man, making sure he had a hand on the line. The smoke was pouring from the hole. He could see that the cribbing was ablaze. The thudding sound came again as some more of the cribbing let go, followed by loosened earth. Anselmo was being decently buried by the same shaft that had killed him. Buck turned his head, inches from Wes' face. "There's yet time to go down," he said.

"Go on, then," said Wes.

"I meant you!" snapped Buck.

Wes heard more cribbing let go. Sparks rose up through the opening, and he bellied hastily backward like an ungainly crab. "Coulter," he said over his shoulder. "If you want that gawd-damned gold, you go down and get it. I'll be happy to lower you."

Buck got back from the smoking, spark-emitting hole. He crawled toward Wes. "How much was there?" he said tensely.

"Thirty iguanas," said Wes. "Maybe three pounds apiece." He wiped the sweat from his face. "About seven thousand dollars' worth at the going rate."

Buck's face fell. "Is that all?" He looked sideways at Wes. "You sure there wasn't more?"

Wes shook his head. "I wasn't going to spend any more time down in that hellhole," he said. "That was the take." He grinned wryly. "At least Anselmo got his share."

The sound of the crackling firewood gathered intensity, and they could hear the steady roaring of the fire as it cremated Anselmo and melted a matrix of pure gold about him. Earthfall after earthfall thudded to the bottom of the shaft. A scarf of smoke drifted in the narrow

128

canyon and rose, staining the view of the clear blue sky high overhead.

Buck felt inside his jacket and brought out a silver flask. He upended it and drank deeply. He lowered the flask and wiped his mouth with his sleeve. "Was that the Killdevil?" he asked quietly.

"Not likely," said Wes. "It was a Jesuit mine. They got run out of Mexico in seventeen sixty-seven. They hid traces of their mines and told the Indians there was a curse upon the mines so that they wouldn't tell anyone else where they were. No one ever had such control over the Indians as the Jesuits did. No one has been down in that mine for well over a hundred years except a double-damned fool like Wes Yardigan, but then I never did have much sense."

"Then it is *not* the Killdevil," said Buck.

Wes shook his head. "Jesus Melgosa was supposed to have worked the Killdevil just before the Civil War," he said.

"We've still got a chance, then," said Buck.

Wes raised his head. "You still want to try for it, then?"

Buck did not speak. He raised the flask again. "We still have the *derrotero*," he said.

Wes looked at the shaft. "And one less partner," he said. "Maybe he took his piece of the *derrotero* down the shaft with him."

"He didn't," said Buck.

Their eyes met. "How did he get that piece he had?" asked Wes.

"It's not important," said Buck.

Wes shook his head. "It is to me. He killed Eusebio Ochoa for it, didn't he?"

Buck fiddled with the flask.

"Buck?" said Wes.

Earth fell heavily within the shaft, sending up a thick gushing of smoke and sparks that began to rise swiftly from the canyon. The gold of the Jesuits was still safe.

Buck stoppered the flask. "Yes," he said quietly. "He killed the old man near Ojo del Muerto. What difference does it make now, Wes? The old man is gone, and Ansel-

129

mo is gone, and we're alive and we have the *derrotero*. Eusebio would have left it for you anyway, most likely."

Wes stood up and began to gather together the gear. There was nothing he could say, nothing he wanted to say. Together they started down the smoke-filled canyon. They did not look back at the buried mine. It was not quite the same. They had left a *patrón* for the Jesuits, a ghostly guardian who would guard the Jesuits' gold until they came back for it. In a sense it was rather fitting, for Anselmo Abeyta, for all his faults, *had* possessed a shabby sort of piousness.

TWELVE

They had hastily moved their camp from the rock cove. The smoke stain against the sky was a sure giveaway for anyone hunting humans or treasure in the Espantosas. No one entered the Espantosas to hunt game. Wes had found a vaulted area where a shallow cave extended back into the rock of the cliff face overlooking the entire area of the cove and the mouth of the slit canyon. He had taken the horses into a deepset box canyon, where there was a little scant grazing but no water.

Buck sat at the rear of the cave. The wind had shifted during the day, and the great heat was gone. Anselmo had left one thing to the partnership—his prediction of the weather.

Buck lighted a cigar. "Don't worry about water," he said. "Anselmo said it would rain."

Wes was cleaning his six-gun. He looked up. "I wasn't just thinking about water," he said.

"Curly will be all right."

Wes nodded. Something alien had sprung up between him and Buck. It might have been coming for quite some time, of course, but now a head was slowly forming. It was becoming increasingly difficult for Wes to speak to

130

Buck, and Wes had never been expert at hiding his feelings. "The sign of an honest heart, chico," Eusebio Ochoa had always said about such a one.

Buck shifted to a more comfortable position. "Anselmo fell into the shaft," he said.

"I know that," said Wes. He reloaded the Colt and closed the loading gate. He wiped the metal with an oily rag.

"By himself," added Buck. "It was an accident, Wes."

Wes stood up, bending his head to keep from hitting the roof of the cave. "Damned careless of him, wasn't it?" he said.

Buck inspected his cigar. "Maybe you would have killed him anyway," he said quietly.

"For Eusebio?" said Wes. "I didn't know he had killed the old man until Anselmo had a minute or two yet to live. If he hadn't fallen into the shaft, I might never have known."

"I meant to tell you," said Buck.

Wes rolled a cigarette. "When?" he asked. "*After* we found Killdevil? Mighty damned convenient for you, Buck."

Buck smiled lazily. "Would you bitch about getting a quarter of Anselmo's share?"

"Providing I would have killed him first," said Wes.

Buck rubbed his crippled leg. He looked up sideways at Wes. "I know that temper of yours, boy. I know what you thought of the old man."

Wes lighted the cigarette. "Had it all figured out, didn't you? Only Anselmo messed up the whole deal by *falling* into that shaft." He looked steadily at Buck.

"What difference does it really make?" asked Buck. "Anselmo has beaten the hangman's noose half a dozen times."

"It wasn't for you to judge," said Wes. "And *execute*," he added.

"He slipped and fell," said Buck. "That's all."

Wes eyed him for a moment and then left the cave. He heard Buck's soft laughter behind him.

The sun was slanting down beyond the western rim of the Espantosas. There was still a faint stain of smoke

131

hanging over the slit canyon—but not enough for anyone to get a fix on it. The shaft would be well plugged by now.

The wind shifted again. Wes quickly raised his head. The faint sound of a human voice came to him. It couldn't be Curly unless he had taken up the habit of talking to himself, but he wasn't the type that even talked to his horse when he was alone. Wes lay flat on the ground and peered between two boulders. Rock clattered beyond his line of vision. Wes uncased his field glasses and focused them on the man who appeared, leading a gray horse. His steeple hat was sharply silhouetted. The thin, cruel face of Luis Galeras swam into view. A few moments later he was followed by the man named Kelly. Then Carl and huge Gonzalo appeared. Wes lowered the glasses. They were on the trail of something all right, judging from their attitudes, but whether it was Wes and his party or that of Luke and Lucy Fairbairn, Wes has no way of knowing. Wes could have gotten at least two of them from where he was hidden. They must have passed right beneath the cliff dwellings. Wes watched them move out of sight. It was possible that they had *not* passed the dwellings. The cold thought crept into Wes' mind.

Luis Galeras stopped beneath a great rock ledge that stood between him and the mouth of the slit canyon. He did not look toward the canyon. The smoke stain had dissipated in the cool wind. The Mexican walked on, followed by the others. They passed within fifty yards of the rock cove but did not stop. In fifteen minutes they had passed out of sight into the mouth of the long and narrow canyon that led toward distant Lonesome Springs. Wes wasted no time in getting back to the cave.

Buck was asleep. He raised his head as Wes gathered his gear. "Where to?" he asked.

"Luis Galeras and his boys just walked past," said Wes.

"So?"

Wes looked at him. "Into the canyon that leads to Lonesome Springs. Supposing they walk right into Curly?"

132

Buck shook his head. "Curly isn't the brightest boy I've ever known, but he isn't likely to be that careless."

"He's got our water," said Wes.

"It's going to rain," said Buck.

There was no use in standing there debating with him. Wes dropped his big canteen beside Buck. "You still might need this," he said.

"What about you? Supposing you don't find Curly?"

"I'll go on to Lonesome Springs. Depend on me to get back with some water, one way or another. Don't try to get back to Ojo del Muerto on just one canteen of water."

"Don't worry," said Buck. "Besides, I'm beginning to like it here."

Wes got his dun. He saw no signs of the Galeras Bunch, but he had to move slowly to keep from giving himself away to them. He didn't know of any shortcuts to Lonesome Springs. The canyon mouth loomed ahead of him, but he had found no signs of hoof tracks.

Long shadows had already fallen from the heights and were already inking in the deeper hollows preparatory to blacking out the canyon before the rising of the moon. Deep hoof marks showed in patches of softer earth. Luis and his boys were riding fast. Likely they, too, needed water. Maybe they didn't have a weather prophet with them. Wes was a mile within the canyon when he saw ahead of him a place where great slabs of decomposing rock had scaled off from the canyon wall to fall and shatter far below. Wes dismounted and led the dun on toward the rocks. Just as he reached the midpoint of the area the dun suddenly shied and blew. Wes raised his head. It was very quiet except for the whispering of the cool wind.

Wes scanned the area behind him and ahead of him. The dun blew vigorously. There was evidently something among the shattered rock piles that was bothering him. The light was getting vague and indistinct, and objects took on unusual appearances, deceptive to the eye.

Wes wet his dry lips. It would be like Luis Galeras to have someone cover his trail, and yet it seemed as though his party had continued on up the darkening canyon. The dun blew again and jerked his head back. Wes withdrew his rifle from its sheath and levered a round into the chamber. The action of the rifle sounded inordinately loud in the quietness. Something was haunting that pile of broken rock. Wes tethered the dun to a scrub tree and worked his way into the tangle. A huge, unbroken slab barred his way. He scaled it and stood on the northern end of it, looking up the darkening canyon. A faint thread of dust hung in the air. The Galeras Bunch were still on the move.

He felt for the makings and as he did so he looked down into a wide hollow, floored with softer earth that had drifted down the steep slope to his right. The patch of earth was deeply pocked with footprints. Wes replaced the makings in his shirt pocket and dropped lightly atop a rock to prevent marring the footprints. He squatted on the rock in the fading light and studied the prints. There were two sets: a booted set and a softer, more rounded and, less distinct set. Both people had been in a hurry. Wes jumped across the tracks and walked along the harder ground. He couldn't tell which set had been made first until he was almost in among the scrub trees and brush of a dense thicket. The softer prints at this point were implanted atop the harder ones. Wes looked about. It was a damned lonely spot. His eyes fell on another set of tracks. A horse this time. He studied them and followed them back the way he had come. There were many hoof tracks in one place and depending from the trunk of a tree were leather reins. He fingered them. They had been sliced through by a sharp knife.

Wes shook his head. The tracks were not absolutely fresh. He picked up a stick and poked through a pile of horse droppings. The outside was crusted, but the interior was not fully dried out. Maybe twenty-four hours, he thought, but that depended upon how hot the sun shone down in here.

He walked back along the line of human tracks. The softer footprints bothered him. The puzzle in his mind did not click into perspective until he looked back and noticed his own prints in the soft earth. *His prints and the other soft prints were exactly the same size and shape!* He knelt

134

to study them. The only difference was in the depth of the prints. The strange prints were deeper, as though the wearer had been running. "Jesus God," he said quietly. *He was wearing Apache moccasins.*

The icy sweat worked down his body. Fear came to ride his back. "Curly?" he said softly. He looked about. The wind had died away. He eyed the strange prints in the dying light. One print seemed a fraction shallower than the other, but he couldn't be sure in that light. Wes rubbed his bristly face. It was the left print. The Apache had been slightly favoring one leg. He walked into the clearing and saw dark blotches on the light-colored earth. He rubbed some of the stained earth between his fingers. "Blood," he said. Wes looked at the far side of the clearing, where broken rock lay strewn about. He padded to it and leaped lightly atop a large rock. He looked down and then quickly turned his head away. The green sour sickness welled up into his throat and mouth. Wes passed a shaking hand across his eyes, and then the foul, sickening smell of escaping body gas came to him, and he whirled, standing spraddle-legged to retch up his guts.

The tears of strain were still in his eyes when he turned once more to look at what remained of Curly Killigrew, the smiling one. The headless bloated body lay sprawled as though overtaken in flight. The head had been completely severed from the body and had either rolled or been kicked ahead of the body to lie upright against a rock, to stare at Wes Yardigan with eyes that did not see. Even as Wes watched the head the last of the fat bluebottle flies rose sluggishly from their feast and flew heavily off to rest for the night, in anticipation of more feasting on the morrow. A great swarm of them arose from the dark pit that had been left when the head had been severed from the body. They settled down again as Wes walked past the corpse.

Wes tied his scarf across his nose and mouth. It looked to him as though Curly had been caught flatfooted by the Apaches, or perhaps only one of them. He had panicked and had run, but he'd never have been able to outrun one of them and he was a lousy runner in any case. It would

135

have been better to have stood and fought it out, because once an Apache has you on the run, he has you cold.

They had stripped Curly of his gunbelt and Colt, as well as his figured boots. His holed and dirty socks had been half pulled off his feet. There was no dignity at all in death for Curly Killigrew. They had left him nothing. Blood had been spattered everywhere. Wes steeled his nerve and looked at that staring head. Had it rolled into that curious position? Had it been placed there as a ghastly joke? *Was it a warning pregnant with deadly symbolism?*

"Few men die natural deaths in the Espantosas," Anselmo Abeyta had always said. He had proved that statement himself.

"Bullshit," said Wes aloud. He made a cigarette and lighted it to get the stink of the headless body out of his nostrils.

The headless bodies found in remote canyons; the many men who have entered the Espantosas and have never been seen again; that nameless something that seems to guard the Lost Killdevil.

"Crap," said Wes.

Wes found a deep crevice. He walked back to the body. "Don't bother to get up," he said. He dragged the swollen, stinking cadaver to the crevice and rolled it in, stepping back to avoid the sudden uprush of flies. He went back to the head and picked it up by the matted curly hair. It seemed extraordinarily heavy, although Curly had never been noted for having a large brain. He placed the head in with the body and hastily kicked loose rock and earth in atop the corpse. He dragged heavier rocks to mound the grave. "There are no coyotes or wolves in the Espantosas," Anselmo had said. Still, Wes didn't want anything digging up that poor body. It had suffered enough indignity.

Wes took off his hat, and as he did so something moved in the darkness of the brush. He whirled, dropping a clawed right hand for a draw. He whipped out the Colt and cocked it in fluid motion, ramming it forward and firing by quick instinct. Echo chased echo in roaring confusion down the dark canyon as he slammed slug after slug into the brush. He stopped firing as he got control of himself. Wes peered into the thickening darkness with powder smoke swirling about his lean face. He began to reload the hot Colt as he padded forward. Something moved just within the brush. He snapped the loading gate shut and thrust out the six-gun. Then he laughed, but there was more relief than mirth in his laughter. A small javelina lay in the brush. Wes pulled the quivering body out into the clearing. Three slugs had driven into the body. "Getting out of practice," he said. A sickening feeling came over him. He knew what had attracted the javelina into the area. As he stood there he heard others grunting and squealing in the darkness and then the sharp pattering of their feet as they ran down the canyon.

Wes walked back to the dun and led it far back into the tangle of brush and shattered rock. Christ, how he wanted to get out of that place already haunted by the unmarked grave of the man who had once been his friend, but Wes was shackled by the darkness. Already the wind had shifted, and there was a damp feeling to the air. Wes walked to where two man-high boulders had leaned together at the top. He crawled in with his rifle and sat down, risking another cigarette. As he lighted it he looked at his Apache mocs. The left leg had been splattered with javelina blood. He wiped at it, but it seemed dry. He pulled off the moccasin and examined it by match light. He picked at the stains with a dirty fingernail. They were as dry as though they had been made some days past, and yet he did not remember noticing them before. Wes examined the sole. It was darkly blotched with what looked like dried blood. He examined the sole of the right moccasin, and it was almost completely covered with the darkness of dried blood.

Wes finished his cigarette and ground it out. It was completely dark now. An eerie, haunting feeling came over him. The moccasins had been good ones. He had traded an old single-barreled Greener shotgun for them before he had gone into the Lagarto. He hadn't stained them with blood in the Lagarto—that, he knew. He ransacked his memory. They had been clean of such stains when he had worn them near Ojo del Muerto, the night he had hurrahed the Galeras Bunch. Wes closed his eyes, struggling with elusive memory. Suddenly he snapped open his eyes. "By God!" he said softly. He had worn them down into the *estufa* mine and he had not stained them, but something now came back to him; as he had held onto Anselmo's wrist in the tense struggle to save the man's life he had been pulled down, and his legs had gone up into the air. He had looked upward and along the line of his left leg. Wes rubbed the sides of his head. The picture came back into his mind. They *had* been stained at that time. Wes remembered, too, when he had gotten out of the shaft, to sit exhausted with his head held in his hands, he had seen his moccasins. They had been stained! *Someone else had been wearing those moccasins.* He stared out into the darkness. Buck Coulter had worn such moccasins when he and Wes had served with the army. To Wes' knowledge he hadn't brought any such footgear along with him into the Espantosas.

A horse whinnied sharply up the canyon. Wes dropped his hands to his rifle. The wind was sharper and was blowing stronger. A hoof struck a stone. A man coughed. Wes pressed back into his hiding niche and almost stopped breathing.

The odor of horses came to him on the wind. They were close—too damned close! Apaches, he thought. If they found him, they'd have him cold, but he'd try to pave hell with a few of them before they got him. They'd never take him alive. It was strange, though. If they were the Apaches who had done in Curly, it wasn't like them to return so soon to the place of death. They would fear that the soul of Curly Killigrew might be still about, speaking in the disguised voice of Bú, the Owl, as he waited for his killers to return so that he might revenge himself on them. They could no longer harm him.

"Christ's blood, Luis!" came the thick voice of Gonzalo Baca. "It's as dark as the pit in here!"

Dark objects moved through the brush in front of Wes' hideout. A horse whinnied sharply, and Wes raised his rifle. He's whiffed me, thought Wes. One by one the four men passed out of sight, heading back out of the canyon. They might have heard him shooting. They had turned back from Lonesome Springs. Perhaps they anticipated the rain, as Anselmo Abeyta had done.

Wes gave the Galeras Bunch half an hour. He crawled out of his nice shelter and as he did so the wind whispered to him, and then the faintest touch of rain struck his face. No fear of needing water now. He went to the dun and bound its hoofs with strips of extra clothing from his saddlebags. The rain came and went, but each time it returned, it was a little heavier. As Gonzalo had said: "Christ's blood, Luis! It's as dark as the pit in here!"

Wes walked slowly. Now and then he looked back up the dark trough of the canyon. It was not from fear but because of what he had left behind him in an unmarked grave, perhaps to be lost from the sight of living men forever. "I used to have a damned good job fixin' windmills onct," Curly had said before he had left for Lonesome Springs. "Not much pay, but you sure could see a lot of nice country whilst you was workin' up there."

THIRTEEN

Staghorn lightning stabbed across the dark and drizzling sky to illuminate the mesa top, revealing Wes and the dun. He must stand out like a lone privy on a West Kansas plain. The lightning flickered out, and Wes set the dun at a fast trot, risking both their necks. The rain came down in a slanting drive, running off the brim of his hat and pattering on his slickered shoulders. "And we needed water," he said wryly.

Thunder drums rumbled in the canyons as Wes rode the dun slantways up a slope that was running with braided streams of silty water Somewhere in the darkness before the coming of the storm he had lost his way. The landmarks were misted in the rain even when the lightning flashed, and in the Espantosas one canyon looked much like another. The lightning cracked flatly with stunning shock, and in the vivid illumination he caught sight of Sangre Cuchillo Peak standing gaunt and rock naked in the streaming rain with a halo of forked lightning dancing wildly about its weather-honed tip. Wes knew then he was too far south to find the canyon where Buck was holed up.

There was a canyon just to the north of him. It was deep in darkness, but in one swift, seconds-long flickering of lighting he knew it as the one they had traveled up in their search for Killdevil, only to find the unsuspected Jesuit mine. Somewhere beneath him must be the great rock vault wherein stood the ancient cliff dwellings. He turned the dun, and as he did so the dun slipped. Wes kicked free of the stirrups and landed on the ground. The dun backed up, shying and blowing in fear. The next shaft of lightning revealed a narrow arroyo with a dark tunnel-like hole at the north end of it. Before the lightning vanished, Wes had seen the marks of a well-worn pathway at the bottom of the cleft.

Wes led the trembling dun between two huge, tip-tilted slabs of rock and tethered it. He took his rifle and went back to the arroyo. He dropped into it. Wes waited for lightning flashes to guide him into the hole. Out of the rain he lighted a candle and saw the flame of it flicker in a strong draft of air pouring from the hole. He had no taste for more tunnels, but he remembered all the stories he had heard about lost mines. Lost men had stumbled into them, taking a minute portion of the ore, then had returned to civilization, but somehow their memories had failed, and none of them were ever able to find their way back again to the lost treasures they had once seen, although they would spend their lives hunting for it. The same virus would attack others, and the legend would grow mightily with the telling.

He stood there in the intermittent light and darkness. The *derrotero* had led them up the canyon in front of the cliff dwellings. Wes had doubted that any mine was in this area, yet they seemed to have stumbled upon the Jesuit mine by dumb luck rather than from any help from the *derrotero*. Was it possible that the *derrotero had* led them to the right area and that they had not recognized it? If the Jesuits had found *oro* in that region, was it not possible that there were other mines as well close by? Mexico's fabulous Lost Tayopa had consisted of a *real de minas,* or group of mines. There was a superstition among lost mine hunters that if one stumbled onto such a tunnel as Wes had found and did not explore it, it would never be found again. It drove him on into the uninviting tunnel.

The floor slanted downward, puddled with rainwater that had run down into the tunnel. He raised the candle. Right in front of him was a slantways wall made of smooth rocks mortared with whitish caliche clay. Faint traces of red paint showed on it, where someone, centuries past, had firmly pressed a paint-wet hand against the lighter wall surface. The bottom of the tunnel was well worn with the passage of many feet. The natural walls showed no marks of drill steel. "By God," said Wes quietly. He had stumbled into the rear entrance to the mass of ancient cliff dwellings that all but filled the great rock vault beneath the edge of the mesa.

Wes walked on, the draft ever stronger on his face. Then lightning traced vividly across the sky, and he could see that he had emerged into a passageway between a row of two-storied buildings. The lightning burned itself out, and the darkness swept in after it like a dark sea tide flooding in on clean white sand.

Something struck rock in the darkness ahead of him. Wes moved softly through the darkness and as the lightning flickered he thought he saw something dark move quickly out of sight up a passageway beside a three-storied tower. He quickly raised his rifle. Maybe I should have a silver bullet, he thought. Wes closed in on the tower in the darkness. He entered the lower room. A ladder was thrust up into the hole in the floor of the second story. He eased himself up it to the next room. In lightning flashes coming through the tiny windows he saw that the floor was littered with a broken ladder and bunches of red and black flint corn. He waited in the darkness but did not hear any sounds except the pattering of the rain on the slope outside, the faint crackling of the lightning, and the low rumbling of the thunder drums.

Wes stepped up on a pile of trash and thrust his rifle through the opening into the third story. He gripped the

141

edge of the hole and started to pull himself up. Something hard ground down on his left hand. He let go and swung from his right hand. His rifle was poked down squarely at his face. He gripped the barrel with his left hand and yanked hard on it, and in the darkness a body struck against his face and chest, driving him to the floor. The body struck the floor and lay still.

Wes snapped a match into life and looked down into the pale face of Lucy Fairbairn. He lighted his candle stub and took an ancient pot to fill it with rainwater. He returned to the room and bathed her face with his bandanna. She opened her eyes and was startled for a moment as she saw him looking down at her. "I thought it was Buck Coulter," she said.

"Why him?" he asked.

She sat up. "I've been waiting for Granddad all day," she said. "I went out onto the terrace some hours ago and saw Buck riding along the slopes. He was alone, but he was looking up here."

"Are you sure, Lucy?"

"I couldn't mistake him," she said. She shivered. "That face and those eyes. I can still see them. Wes, he was *hunting* for something, like a great cat."

"Where's Luke?" asked Wes.

She hesitated. "He went up the canyon," she said.

"Hunting for Killdevil?"

She shook her head and looked away.

"Tailing my bunch, then?"

"Yes," she said. "I tried to keep him from going. Wes, he isn't right in the head. There was nothing I could do to stop him. The only way to keep him out of these mountains is to have him committed and locked up, and I can't bring myself to do that."

"He can lead you to your own death," said Wes quietly.

"If he runs into Buck or Anselmo Abeyta or that grinning Curly Killigrew . . ." Her voice trailed off hopelessly.

"He won't find either of those last two alive," said Wes.

She looked quickly at him. "How did they die?"

"Anselmo *fell* into a mine shaft. Curly was murdered by an *Apache*," he said.

Her eyes narrowed. "You sound as though that was not

the real way they died," she said. "Tell me the truth, Wes."

"What difference does it make now?" he said.

"It makes a difference to you, Wes. What are you holding back from me?"

Wes stood up. "Maybe the old man holed up in the storm," he said. He helped her to her feet.

"You got through it," she said.

He looked down at her. "Do you have any coffee?" he asked.

She studied his face and then nodded. She led the way through a winding, trash-littered passageway into a room at the rear of the dwellings. She took the candle from Wes' hand and lighted a small lantern. "It's all right," she said over her shoulder. "No light can be seen in here from the outside. The smoke rises up the back of the rock vault and dissipates, so that one can hardly see it."

"Very clever. You've been here before, then?"

She nodded. She lighted a small fire and placed the coffee pot close to it. A repeating rifle leaned against the wall, and she wore a holstered Colt. Wes knew she knew how to use both weapons. Luke Fairbairn had been a crack rifle shot in his day, serving in Berdan's First United States Sharpshooters during the war, although he had not been a young man even then.

She sat and watched the fire grow, and the flickering light danced across her lovely face. "I'm all Granddad has left," she said, almost as though she were talking to herself. "I can't stop him from coming into the Espantosas alone, so I have to come with him. Maybe the Lost Killdevil is all he has left to believe in. I've been wondering how long I'll have to keep on with his obsession for Killdevil."

"You've got your own life to live," said Wes. "Whatever duty or loyalty you owed to him, you've paid off in full. If he won't stop in this madness of his, you'd better get out of these mountains while you can."

She shook her head. "I've come this far with him. I can't leave without him. Will you go and look for him? Or do you owe all your loyalty to Buck Coulter?"

"I'll look for him," he said. "Buck Coulter is my friend,

and I do owe him some loyalty, as I owe loyalty to all my friends. Is that enough for you, Lucy?"

She would not look at him. She was wise enough to know, even at her years, that a woman does well not to interfere between a man and his friends or at least his best friend.

A deep loneliness crept into Wes as he watched her sitting by the fire. He had lost his own family when he had hardly been able to understand the full measure of the tragedy. He had parted with Eusebio Ochoa because the old man had insisted on staying in the Espantosas, until he had met his own violent death in them. Wes had left Lucy because he had had nothing to offer her to live in but a pair of worn saddlebags and the sky of the lonely Lagarto Desierto for a roof. Anselmo Abeyta had meant nothing to him, and the loss of Curly Killigrew had not been a great shock. Wes' friendship with Buck Coulter had been severely strained, and the impact of it had left him a little numb in his feelings. Now, it seemed, his only real tie with Buck Coulter was a business deal, formed on a handshake and deep mutual trust, to find the Killdevil. The handshake had seemed firm and lasting; the mutual trust no longer so. The Killdevil no longer seemed to really matter. It was the oncoming loss of Buck Coulter as his friend that mattered to Wes, and yet it seemed as though there were nothing he could do about it, just as Lucy could do little about her relationship with her grandfather.

"You're awfully far away," she said quietly.

His head snapped up. He had been lost in his thoughts. As he looked at her again he felt once more the full measure of his deep loneliness. Perhaps he had never possessed Lucy Fairbairn and he was almost sure he never would. He was a loser, a man who walked through life always alone. "I'm sorry," he said. "Maybe I did spend too much time out on the Lagarto."

She shook her head. "That's all in your mind," she said. "You're probably better off for it."

He shrugged. "I haven't figured that one out yet, Lucy."

She handed him a cup of coffee and wisely changed the subject. "Granddad was beginning to think he finally had a clue to Killdevil. He didn't have a piece of that *derro-*

tero, but after all his years in the Espantosas hunting for Killdevil he had put down one clue after another and fact after fact and had fashioned what he called a *conocimiento* complete enough so that one more trip into these mountains would be his last, and he'd find the Killdevil. He became panicky when he heard that Buck Coulter might have a lead to the lost mine. When he found out that Buck had sent Anselmo and Curly after you, he was almost positive that Buck was really onto something. The trouble was that until Granddad had learned that Buck was after the Killdevil, too, he had always trusted Buck and put some of his confidences into him. I guess Granddad had talked too much, and Buck had figured out that Granddad had worked out a *conocimiento* or that he had valuable material about it."

"Luke was just building up something in that suspicious mind of his," said Wes.

"Perhaps," she said. "My father had located a piece of the *derrotero,* or at least he *thought* he had. He would not let Granddad go up into the mountains with him, but instead he took Marcos Padilla."

"And your father never came back."

She nodded. A shadow of sorrow and loneliness seemed to pass swiftly over her face. "Wes, that boy never killed my father. Whoever did kill Dad had figured Dad had the piece of *derrotero,* but Dad had given it to Marcos, who managed to escape with it."

Wes shaped a cigarette. "Why are you so sure Marcos did not kill your father?"

"Marcos loved my father. Marcos was a simple young man in that the gold meant nothing to him, but my father's friendship meant a great deal. Marcos feared the Espantosas as most Mexicans do. I think that the fact that Marcos did go with my father into these mountains shows how much he must have loved my father. I saw Marcos for a little while when he was in Eden City jail. He wanted to tell me something, but Buck Coulter was always within earshot. When I said good-bye to Marcos, I could see that the spirit was dying within him. He acted as though he would never see me again and he was right because he was found dead in his cell the next morning."

145

Wes lighted the cigarette. "Frightened into suicide."

"I don't know," she said. "No one will ever know Either way, Buck Coulter got the piece of *derrotero*."

He looked sideways at her. "Just what do you mean by 'either way,' Lucy?" he asked quietly.

Her eyes held his steadily, and it was Wes who first looked away.

"You know what I mean," she said. "For God's sake, Wes! Don't trust Buck Coulter any further! He isn't the man you once knew and loved! He is capable of doing anything to those who stand in his way! Even *you*, Wes!"

Wes drained his coffee cup and stood up. "Did Luke have his *conocimiento* with him when he left here?" he said.

She studied his taut face for a moment. "Yes," she said.

"If anything happens, do you think you can find your way out of the Espantosas?"

"The horses and the burro are picketed not far from here. I can find my way to Ojo del Muerto."

"Travel at night. Don't make any fires. Don't panic."

She looked up at him. "What makes you think I'll have to leave here alone?"

Wes shrugged. He drew her up to him and looked down into her lovely face, and then he kissed her, just once, and was gone with his catlike tread. She stood there in the flickering firelight, touching her face where his whiskers had scraped, but it was not because of the pain of it. She had been kissed by others before, and Wes Yardigan as well, but never quite like that. She had learned something new as well. When Wes Yardigan had stubbornly gone out into the Lagarto, part of her had gone with him. This time it seemed as though her whole heart had gone with him, and she knew she would never be the same again, whether or not he ever returned to her.

FOURTEEN

Wes walked down the long slope in the intermittent flashing of the lightning. Now and again water slopped over

146

he feet of his moccasins as he waded through braided streams running inches deep with silty water. Maybe the old man had just holed up to stay out of the wet. It gave Wes an uneasy feeling to think of the yawning muzzle of the big-bored Sharps Luke carried. Men usually shot first and asked questions later in the Espantosas.

He turned to head for the ridge that was slightly southeast of the cliff dwellings. It wasn't very far from there to the mouth of the slit canyon. Likely Luke had been nosing around up there. Water sheeted across the naked rock slopes and cascaded from the heights in feathery streams tinted silver by the flashing lightning. It was the type of weather during which Noah might have wondered if he were going to get his ark done in time. He saw the mouth of the rock alcove in one vivid, ear-shattering bolt of lightning. He felt his way into it in the thick darkness after the flashing of the lightning. Lightning forked across the sky in a splitting discharge, and Wes stopped short in quick horror. The naked body of Luke Fairbairn lay flat on its back with the arms outflung. Luke stared at Wes with eyes that did not see. His mouth was crookedly agape above the tobacco-stained beard, and his yellow teeth seemed to protrude inordinately far from the thin, drawn-back lips. Water had puddled up as high as his ears.

The lightning flickered out, plunging canyon and mesa into utter darkness. The rain drummed down more intensely. Wes fought to get control of his nerves. In the next lightning illumination he knelt beside the old man and rolled him over. He turned his head aside, and the green sickness welled sourly up in his throat. The back of the skull was caved in, and a bluish hole showed between the thin shoulderblades. Apaches, thought Wes. It was obvious. They had killed from ambush, as they liked to do; the body was stripped, and the fine Sharps rifle was gone; the head was caved in so that the vengeful spirit of the dead would not pursue them. Wes stood up. Two things didn't fit the pattern. Luke Fairbairn was considered by many to be touched. There had been times in his past history when he had passed through hostile Apache country and had not been harmed because the Apaches had

147

thought him *mind-gone-far,* and they would not harm such a person, thinking him as being protected by the gods. Even so, if they had not thought this of him, there was another factor that entered the matter. When the drums of the Thunder People rolled in the gorges and the arrows of Ittindi, the Lightning, flashed across the streaming skies, no Apache would be on the prowl for unsuspecting victims. Someone had killed Luke from behind and had made it *look* like an Apache killing, the same way it had appeared that Curly Killigrew had been murdered.

"Buck Coulter," said Wes Yardigan into the streaming darkness, and Ittindi answered by hurling a great shaft of lightning clear across the Espantosas to strike with savage force against Sangre Cuchillo Peak. "Unless it was the Galeras Bunch," added Wes lamely as darkness came again. He stepped back and something rolled beneath his left moccasin. He picked up an empty cartridge hull and as the lightning flashed he could read the caliber stamped on the rim of the cartridge base. ".38/56," he said quietly.

Wes hoisted the old man to his shoulders and plodded out of the rock alcove and down the long slope of the ridge past the slitted mouth of the canyon where they had found the Jesuit mine and where Anselmo Abeyta was buried with his gold. At least Anselmo had funds to pay his way into the hereafter; old Luke would have nothing but his gingery personality to grease his way. There was little feeling for Luke within Wes. The old man had lived his allotted time. He had been living on borrowed time every trip he had made into the Espantosas. The inevitable had happened to him, like the victim in a Greek tragedy. The Espantosas' appetite for blood was being well fed this week. Wes wondered when they would be sated.

Wes placed the old man in a tiny, windowless room at the bottom of a three-tiered tower at the far end of the dwellings where Lucy was staying. He walked slowly to where she was and softly called out to her. She could shoot as fast and as accurately as the average man. She returned his call, and he took her into his arms as he entered the room. The fire was marked by a thick bed of ashes wherein a suspicious red eye winked now and then

148

like a one-eyed witch. "He's dead," she said. She pressed her face against his chest. Wes picked her up and placed her on her bed. "How did he die?" she asked.

Wes looked away. This was worse than discovering the body.

"I know," she said. "Like all the others. What is it they say about the Espantosas?"

"Few men die natural deaths in the Espantosas," he said. "It is a legend, but it is true. I lost my family that way when I was only five years old. The Espantosas took Eusebio Ochoa from me. They take everything from me, it seems."

"And Buck Coulter?" she asked.

"He's still alive," he said quietly.

"But they have taken him from you just the same."

He had no answer for that one. He stood up and peeled off his slicker and unbuckled his gunbelt. He peeled off his soaked moccasins and placed them near the fire. Despite the horrors of the past few days a vague sort of peacefulness had come over him. He knew it would not last. Peacefulness had little chance against the brooding spirit of the Espantosas. He would savor the peacefulness for a little time at least.

"Where will you go when you leave here?" she said.

"I'm not sure," he said.

"If you find the Lost Killdevil, will it make a difference?"

"How can I answer that?" he asked.

"What of Buck Coulter?"

Wes shrugged. "He might find what he wants, or what he *thinks* he wants. I don't know."

She shook her head. "No, Wes. He never will."

"You seem almighty sure of that, Lucy."

"You know it as well as I do," she said.

"Well, I've got my own life to think about," he said.

"That's it exactly, Wes. You're coming to your senses at last!"

He looked sideways at her with a crooked smile. "There ever speaks womanhood to man," he said in a droll voice.

The faint crackling of the lightning came to them, mingled with the dull rumbling of the thunder drums.

Neither of them spoke for a time but there seemed to be a silent communication between them. "Maybe Granddad has found his happiness at last," she said after a time. "I don't think he ever had it upon this earth. He wasn't the kind of man who wanted to die peacefully in bed with his family and friends gathered about him. He told me once when I was very small that he wished he had died in the war. It was as though he was living at that time the kind of experiences that were food and drink to him and that everything thereafter was dross."

Wes nodded. "I think I know what he meant."

"Perhaps that is what bothers Buck Coulter," she said. He had no answer for that one.

"God help Granddad," she said softly, "and God forgive me for saying so, but it was better this way."

He came to her in the semidarkness, which was lighted now and then by the faint flickering of the fire as it arose a little from the embers and ashes and then died away once again. He drew her close. She shivered, but it wasn't from the cold, for it was warm and cozy in that room built in centuries past and fireless for hundreds of years. They did not speak. There was no need to speak. They had found each other at long last. The responsibility for the old man was gone from her young shoulders, and now she was needed by another man, a younger man who was not of her blood. It was Wes Yardigan who wanted and needed her now as she wanted and needed him. Let the dead bury the dead . . .

The rain had stopped, and it was very quiet when at last Wes opened his eyes. She was sleeping soundly. He covered her and then got dressed. In the faint light of a match he wrote charcoal message to her on the whitish surface of the wall. She was to remain there until he came back for her.

To hell with Buck Coulter and his lust for the gold of Killdevil! The thought filled Wes' mind as he returned for the dun and led it across the ridge to where Buck's sorrel had been picketed. The search for Killdevil was over as far as Wes was concerned. All Wes wanted to do was to get Lucy out of the accursed Espantosas. He didn't have a centavo to his name—less than what he had had when he had gone out onto the Lagarto to seek his fortune, as it said in the fairy tales. Christ, he thought, now I'll *have* to get a good job. He had one advantage over Buck—the love of a woman like Lucy Fairbairn.

FIFTEEN

Buck was sitting up in his blankets with a rifle in his hands when Wes entered the cave after he had given the agreed-upon whistle signal, one they had always used between them in their scouting days. "By God," said Buck. "You took your time!"

It was almost dawn. Wes took off his wet hat and peeled off his slicker. "You've got your water, Buck," he said.

"What about Curly?"

Wes sat down and peeled off his moccasins. He could not look at Buck. Wes had never been one to carry off deception. His emotions usually showed on his face unless he made a Spartan effort not to let them show. "Dead," said Wes. "Apaches."

Buck shook his head. "Poor Curly," he said.

Wes nodded. "From the looks of it, he had only seconds to live before he knew what was after him."

Buck glanced sideways at Wes. "How so?"

Wes unbuckled his gunbelt and withdrew the cartridges and the Colt. "Tracks," he said laconically. "Curly ran when he should have stood. He never had a chance. Head cut clean off. Looked like one good swipe."

"Luck of the game," said Buck.

Wes wiped his Colt with an oily rag. "I think we've run out our string," he said.

"Why so, boy?"

"We lost the Jesuit gold. Anselmo and Curly are gone. Isn't that enough to convince you?"

"We've got a clear field now, Wes! The Galeras Bunch

151

has pulled foot. It's just the two of us now, like old times. We can make it together, boy!"

Wes pulled on dry levis and shirt as Buck sliced the last of the bacon into the spider. Buck placed the frying pan over the embers and fed the fire with twigs. "I have the damnedest feeling that we've been looking in the wrong direction," he said over his shoulder.

Wes walked to his boots and picked them up. "It's no use, Buck," he said. The boot leather was damp. He looked down at them.

"Remember how we talked up in my rooms at the Territorial House, boy? Look, Wes! We can't quit now. I need you, and you need me. We need each other for this search. Neither one of us can make it alone."

"Partners to the death," said Wes dryly.

"You said we could pull out of Eden City if we made a strike. You wanted me to go in with you on that spread in the Chiricahuas. Well, *I'm* still for it! We made a deal, didn't we, boy?"

"It's just these bloody mountains that have gotten to me," said Wes. He suddenly realized that the boots were not his. They were Buck's boots. The soles were water-soaked, and fresh mud was caked in at the seam, where soles and uppers met. He remembered what Lucy had said: "I couldn't mistake him. That face and those eyes. I can still see them. Wes, he was *hunting* for something, like a great cat."

"Jesus Melgosa always insisted that his mine was not far from live water," said Buck. "No one ever knew how far that was or what spring of live water he was referring to. Right?"

"Right," said Wes. "But Jesus Melgosa never handed out any free or accurate information that I ever heard about."

"There are only three live water sites in the Espantosas," said Buck eagerly. "Lonesome Springs, Tonto Seep, and Ojo del Muerto. Are there any diggings around Lonesome Springs?"

Wes pulled on his own boots. "Years ago. Played out right after the war. Nothing there, Buck."

"What about Tonto Seep?"

Wes shook his head. "Absolutely nothing."

"That leaves Ojo del Muerto!" said Buck triumphantly.

There was no expression on Wes' face. "There may have been live water holes that have gone dry since the time of Jesus Melgosa."

Buck smashed a fist down on his good thigh. "For Christ's sake, boy! Here I'm giving you a real lead for once, and you can't see it!"

Wes began to dry his cartridges. He remembered something he had noticed on the piece of *derrotero* he had seen out on the Lagarto, something so indefinite he had almost forgotten about it.

"Eusebio Ochoa was killed near Ojo del Muerto," said Buck. "No one knew these mountains better than he did. And who knew more about the Lost Killdevil than Old Eusebio? Doesn't *that* indicate anything to you?"

"Only that he was murdered," said Wes. "You're burning the bacon."

Buck became very quiet, but Wes would not turn to look at him. Wes had never seen anything that would make him think Ojo del Muerto possibly held the secret of the Lost Killdevil, and then something stabbed into his mind like a barbed shaft. There had once been a marking where the two pieces of hide had been torn apart. That marking had looked vaguely familiar when Wes had studied the *derrotero* in Buck's rooms at the Territorial House. Something like the ragged half of a figure 8. Jesus God, he thought. No wonder Eusebio had been hunting around Ojo del Muerto! Maybe he had been close to Killdevil at the time of his death. *Maybe he had even found Killdevil!*

"So," said Buck, as he handed Wes a plate of bacon, "we can head back to Ojo del Muerto and start the hunt all over."

Wes sat down on a rock. "You might as well know," he said quietly, "that I've seen and talked with Lucy Fairbairn. Old Luke is dead. Murdered by Apaches, from the looks of it."

"Good God!" said Buck. He stared incredulously at Wes. "Apaches? Are you positive?"

153

"I think so," said Wes.

Buck shook his head. "And after all I've taught you, too. You said the same thing about Curly. Don't you know for sure if it was the Apaches who did the both of them in?"

"I said I *thought* so," said Wes. "Pass the bread."

"What about the girl? That poor kid! Is she all right?"

Wes looked quickly at Buck. There was complete concern evident on Buck's face and in his tone of voice. "I want to get her out of these damned mountains," Wes said.

"Of course you will!" said Buck. "God's blood, boy! Did you think I was against your doing that? That's first, of course! But listen to me for a minute. We've got to go back by way of Ojo del Muerto in any case. You're not fool enough to pass up a chance at Killdevil are you? By God, Wes! I feel it in my bones! We're so close to it now!"

Wes emptied his plate and placed it on the ground. Buck tossed him a cigar and held out a smoldering twig to light it. Wes drew in the good tobacco smoke. There was nothing Wes could do now to bring back Eusebio Ochoa. Anselmo and Curly had placed their lives at stake in the big game to find fabulous riches and they had lost, as Jim Fairbairn and his father had done. It was part of the harsh rules by which the game was played.

"You can have that spread, Wes," said Buck. "I have a feeling the deal for that is off between you and me, but that's the way it should be."

"Meaning?" said Wes.

"You and Lucy of course! I'm not blind. Maybe it's just as well. I've gotten used to city life. I doubt if I'd ever be able to work at ranching, or at least my heart would not be in it." Buck poked the fire and filled two coffee cups. "That isn't to say I won't come out and stay with you at times. A little fishing—a fat buck or two in the fall. I can watch your kids grow up tall and strong like their father. Real men of the west, boy!"

Wes spat to one side. "For Christ's sake, Buck!" he said. "You're talking to Wes Yardigan, not to Curly Killigrew."

Buck grinned slyly. "How well I know," he said. "You'll make one more try for the Killdevil, then?"

Wes nodded. "You win. You always do."

A faint and fleeting shadow fled across Buck's lean face. "Look, boy, I've got to make it. No one knows better than you. I need your help, and it isn't as though it will cost you a price. Odds are that we'll make it this time. Is it a deal?"

"It's a deal," agreed Wes.

Buck smiled. "I knew you'd never let me down. You won't regret it, Wes."

Wes had had little choice. Likely Buck didn't know how much Wes knew and suspected—or at least he wasn't letting on that he did. Evidence was strong that Buck had killed Anselmo, Curly, and old Luke, but it was purely circumstantial evidence. If Buck ever suspected how much Wes really knew, the odds were that neither Wes nor Lucy would live to get out of the Espantosas, and yet Wes could not, even for the life of him, believe that Buck Coulter had killed those three men or that he might be considering getting rid of Wes once he got his hands into the gold of the Killdevil.

"Let's move out," said Buck. "Andele!"

The sun was up as they rode toward the cliff dwellings. Here and there shallow pools of water dotted the soaked ground, but already the thirsty soil was greedily sucking in the moisture. Half a day of sunlight would dry up all the surface water. Buck went to look for the Fairbairn horses while Wes climbed the slope to the cliff dwellings. She met him on the ancient terrace and came to his arms. "Is that Buck Coulter down there?" she asked him.

"Yes, Lucy," said Wes. "We're getting out of here." He did not want to tell her about the stop at Ojo del Muerto to continue the hunt for Killdevil—not yet at least. "Get your things," he added. "I've got to take care of your granddad."

She nodded. "Maybe this is the way he always wanted it."

Wes walked to the ancient tower, where Luke's body lay in the lowest room. Wes did not look into the room. He swung himself up to the doorway of the second-floor room and ripped loose a juniper log rafter from the crum-

155

bling ceiling. He rammed at the floor until it collapsed into the lower room, covering the body of Luke Fairbairn. A gray film of finely powdered dust arose above the tower. Wes dropped to the ground. "Sleep well, old man," he said softly. "Your troubles are over."

Buck waited at the edge of the terrace with the two Fairbairn horses. "The burrito must have strayed," he said.

"We won't need him," said Wes. He saddled one of the two horses and made a pack to be slung on the back of the other. He gave Lucy a leg up into her saddle, and they rode after Buck Coulter down the long sunlit canyon. Only once did she glance up at the tower that was the tomb of Luke Fairbairn and then she looked away. She would not look at Buck Coulter, almost as though he did not exist.

Now and then Wes would glance at Buck. Buck rode with a cigar jutting from his mouth and his eyes half closed, oblivious to both Lucy and Wes. How much did he really know?

There was no sign of life in the great canyon that lay below Sangre Cuchillo Peak. The patch of greenery that marked Ojo del Muerto was visible against the gray-brown flank of the towering peak. A lone, ragged-winged hawk hung motionless high above them as they rode out into the canyon. There was a feeling of utter loneliness about the huge trough that cut through the Espantosas. There wasn't a friendly thread of ranch house smoke or the reflection of bright sunlight on rain-washed windows. No windmill whirred in the fresh breeze that was sweeping through the canyon. Not a road or a fence could be seen in all that vastness. The trail they followed was almost indistinct, so faint was it. The fact of the matter was that while men passed through the Espantosas, they never stayed there any longer than they had to stay except for those who left their bodies there while their souls fled precipitately to happier areas.

SIXTEEN

Shadows had drifted down the rugged sides of Sangre Cuchillo Peak to fill in the hollows about Ojo del Muerto. The wind had died away with the coming of the dusk, and only the very tips of the cottonwoods and willows moved uneasily, a sign of oncoming rain. The horses whinnied and increased their pace as they scented the fresh water.

Wes looked at Lucy. "From here on," he said with a smile, "we're on the way out."

The rifle cracked flatly from the deep shadows beside the first pool. Wes' dun had sidestepped and shied a little, and as he threw up his handsome head the bullet struck it. As the dun went down Wes kicked loose from the stirrups and landing spraddle-legged. "Ride!" he yelled at Lucy. His Winchester was pinned beneath the dun. Wes sprinted for cover. Buck bent low in the saddle and ripped his short-barreled Colt from its half-breed holster inside his coat. He fired right over Wes' head to keep the rifleman down. Gun flashes spurted from the thick greenery as Wes went to ground beyond the third and deepest pool. Wes caught a momentary glimpse of a steeple hat banded with coin silver. He slammed a wild shot at it from his Colt.

Buck rode into the shelter of the trees down the slope from Wes. "Vamanos!" he yelled at Wes as he ripped his Winchester .38/56 from the saddle scabbard. Slugs whipped through the brush, cutting off twigs and leaves. Wes bellied along feeling utterly naked. Boots thudded on the ground beyond him. Wes shot a glance over his shoulder to see the man named Carl running toward him firing his rifle as he did so. Buck leaped clear of the brush and fired twice from the hip. Carl fell forward. His rifle plunged into the third pool. He rolled over once and lay still amid the wreathing gunsmoke.

"You all right, boy?" yelled Buck.

"Keno!" replied Wes. He elbow-worked his way unseen

out onto the man-wide ledge that skirted just above the third pool.

"I'll hold them off, Wes!" yelled Buck. "Pull foot, amigo!"

Wes took the hint and lay flat. The gunfire had died away. Powder smoke drifted slowly through the trees. Wes watched the brush beyond the second pool. Slowly he pushed forward his Colt, resting his arm on the ground and gripping his gunwrist with his left hand. He heard Buck stampede his horse down the slope. A huge man stood up and peered across the third pool toward where he had heard the hoofbeats. It was Gonzalo Baca. "Come on, Luis!" he yelled in his thick voice. "They have run!" He ran slowly out into the open.

"For the love of God, Gonzalo!" yelled Luis. "No!"

Wes fired once. Gonzalo died with a bullet in his head before the echo of Luis' warning had died away. Bullets slashed through the brush and keened from the rocks about Wes. Lead shards lacerated his left cheek. He could not go back, and both riflemen were ahead of him. He looked up the steep rock face above the third pool. It was the only way to go, and he knew he'd never make it without getting a slug between the shoulderblades.

"Go on, boy!" yelled Buck.

Wes thrust his Colt into its holster and leaped upward, stabbing with his boot toes into crevices and clawing for holds with his hands. A rataplan of gunfire came from the trees where Buck was concealed. He was covering Wes. Wes reached the top. A slug tore off his left boot heel, numbing his leg. He dragged himself toward cover. Boots thudded on rock. Kelly jumped into sight, rifle in hand. Wes ripped out his Colt and fired without even leveling the handgun. Kelly staggered with the shock of the heavy .44/40 slug, but the man had guts. He fired at Wes. Rock shards spurted up into Wes' face as he fired again. Kelly fell sideways over the brink and plunged to his death in the pool below.

Wes scrubbed a hand across his tear-filled eyes.

"Wes!" yelled Buck. "Move! Get out of the way!"

Dimly Wes could see a fourth man running toward him. It must be Luis Galeras. Galeras raised his rifle, and

Wes dived cleanly from the brink, hoping to God the water below was deep enough so that he would not break his fool neck. Even as he touched the water with his fingertips he heard two shots fired from above him. He went down deep, deep into the cold water, and his hands touched something smooth and rounded like a six-inch pipe. Wes felt about with his hands for a moment. He turned his body and braced his feet on the rounded surface to give him impetus to rise to the surface far above him. He shot up toward the surface and broke water, half expecting a slug to meet him. He treaded water. High above him Buck Coulter stood in the last of the dying light looking down at him. "Took you long enough to come back up, boy!" he called. "What'd you find down there? A mermaid?"

Wes swam slowly to the rim of the pool and crawled out. Four men dead in not more than ten minutes. Buck and Wes had wiped out the Galeras Bunch forever.

Buck limped down the rocky pathway. "Just like the old days!" he crowed. "We still make the best man-killing team in the business, boy!"

Wes felt his lacerated cheek. It had been too damned close for comfort. "Lucy! Lucy!" he called.

Buck was reloading his rifle. "When we find Killdevil," he said, "I can pay off my debts and get into politics. I'll back you for sheriff in the next election. With me running the political end and you taking the active part out in the county, we'll be a great team. What do you say, boy?"

"I'd like to die in bed," said Wes dryly. He limped to meet Lucy.

It was fully dark by the time they had roped the dead bodies and hauled them far down the slope to dump them into a deep crevice and cover them with rocks. It took longer to haul the dead dun away from the springs. The buzzards would strip and gut it soon enough.

Buck was preparing a fire as Lucy and Wes walked toward him. He picked up a short length of wood and flipped it into the air. The heavy-bladed knife he held in his right hand swung up to strike with vicious force at the end of the billet, slicing it cleanly into two pieces. The sight brought something back to Wes. Curly Killigrew had been running panic-stricken when he had been overtaken by his pursuer and neatly decapitated by just such a knife and such a powerful blow.

Buck looked sideways at Wes and seemed to read something on his face. "What's wrong, boy?" he said.

"Nothing, really," answered Wes. "I was just thinking about starting a fire here. Somehow it doesn't seem the right thing to do at Ojo del Muerto."

Buck laughed. "Who is there to bother us now? The dead certainly won't bother us. We can eat the last of our food and get some sleep. At the crack of dawn we can start hunting for Killdevil. It's bound to be within a short distance of the springs."

"No one has ever found it," said Wes. "Not since the time of Jesus Melgosa. That is, unless someone *did* find it and never lived to talk about it."

Buck glanced up at Wes. He narrowed his eyes a little. "Well, we'll find it. Somehow I feel that we just can't miss." He fed split wood to the fire. "It's around here, Wes. I know it."

"How did you figure that out, Mr. Coulter?" said Lucy quietly.

Both men were startled. She had hardly spoken a word for hours. "I have ways," said Buck.

"Yes, Mr. Coulter," she said. "You have ways. Granddad had a feeling that Killdevil was back this way."

Buck shrugged. "Then, what was he doing east of the canyon?"

"He wasn't sure."

"He was tailing us," said Buck.

"Even so," she said. "He said he thought Killdevil just might be back this way and he told me he planned to search around here when we left that canyon and the way was clear. Mr. Coulter, I had never heard him say before that he thought Killdevil was near Ojo del Muerto. Isn't it possible that he was the only person, with the possible exceptions of Jesus Melgosa and Eusebio Ochoa, who might know that? The only *living* person?"

Buck got to his feet. "Just what are you driving at, Miss Fairbairn?" he asked in a low voice.

"Granddad had a *conocimiento* with him when he left

me. It's possible it might have had information on the Lost Killdevil."

"Possible?" said Buck. "But you don't know, do you?"

"The *conocimiento* was not on his body when it was found," persisted Lucy.

Buck shrugged. "Perhaps the Apaches took it," he said.

"No," said Lucy. "It would have meant nothing to them."

Buck looked away from her. "Maybe Wes got it," he suggested.

"No," she said firmly. "He did not."

"He told you that?"

"He never said a word about it, Mr. Coulter, and what is more, he didn't have to."

"You're a trusting little soul," Buck sneered.

She looked full into his eyes. "I am," she said quietly, "to those I *can* trust."

Buck looked at Wes. "And you?" he said softly. "How do you feel, boy?" He studied Wes' face for a full moment, and there was no need for an answer. He knew Wes Yardigan probably far better than Wes knew him. Buck looked down at the crackling fire. His rifle was leaning against a rock fifteen feet away, and his Colt was holstered within his buttoned coat. He knew well enough that if there was any living man who might match him in a draw it was the man standing behind him. Wes Yardigan had been but an eager lad when he had come to Buck to learn the manifold tricks of the trade—of fast draws and deadly shooting, of scouting and Indian fighting—the tricks by which a man survives in a killing business. The *boy* had learned well, perhaps all too well. He had had a fine teacher, thought Buck wryly.

Pictures sped through Wes' mind. Of Anselmo Abeyta screaming out his terror as he dangled in the smoky shaft of the old Jesuit mine, clearing his conscience before his death by confessing that he had murdered Eusebio Ochoa. Of Curly Killigrew, the rather simple-minded smiling one, who had been left to feast the bluebottle flies. Of the naked, aged body of old Luke Fairbairn staring up at Wes Yardigan with eyes that did not see, while the back of his skull was a smashed-in horror to the eye.

161

Buck slowly turned. "No use, eh, boy?"

Wes shook his head.

"You aim to take me in, Wes?"

The wind was rising a little, bringing a faint spit of cold rain with it.

"You can take two of the horses," said Wes. "The border is only forty miles away. I'll give you twenty-four hours before I turn you in."

"I need a drink, boy."

"Go ahead," said Wes.

Buck felt inside his coat, keeping his eyes on Wes. He knew if he made one false move, it could be a fatal one. Buck withdrew his expensive silver flask. He drank deeply and held out the flask to Wes. "You want to kill it?" he said. Wes shook his head. Buck drained it and then carelessly flipped the flask into the nearest pool. "Where are the snows of yesteryear?" he said quietly. He looked sideways at Wes with half a smile. "You won't help me find Killdevil? Take the time to help me, Wes. I'll need the money to live, even in Mexico."

Wes shook his head.

There was a knowing smile on the face of the older man. "But you think you know where it is, eh? Well, it's getting on toward midnight. Five hours more. Then the golden coach turns back into a pumpkin. I hope to God my sorrel doesn't turn into a rat. That would be the cruelest blow of all."

The rain began to mist down and then to patter steadily on the dry leaves and the ground. Smoke and steam arose from the fire and drifted over the dark pools of water. Buck squatted by the fire and idly fed wood to it. "Go on, boy," he said quietly. "Change those wet clothes and take Lucy home."

Buck did not look up again as Wes and Lucy rode past him toward the out trail. The rain slashed down heavily and put out the fire. Buck stood up, wreathed in the smoke and steam, a tall, lonely figure of a man. He took out his cigar case and opened it. One broken cigar was in it. "Figures," said Buck dryly. He broke it fully in half and lighted one piece of it and then limped slowly into the shelter of the dark woods.

SEVENTEEN

They reached Tonto Seep just before midnight, riding through a chilling drizzle of rain. Wes led the way to a shallow cave and found enough dry wood within it to start a fire. He placed a saddle blanket on the ground for Lucy to sit upon and draped one of his blankets about her shivering shoulders. She looked up at him as he did so. "He thinks you know where Killdevil is, Wes," she said.

He looked sideways at her with a slow grin. "Why," he said quietly, "I think so, too."

"Wes! You're pulling my leg!"

He looked down at her shapely, booted legs. "I'm a gentleman," he reminded her.

"Well, do you know where it is or not?"

Wes shaped a cigarette and looked thoughtfully into the fire. "Buck was right in saying that we must return toward Ojo del Muerto to find the Lost Killdevil. Evidently your grandfather had already figured it out. Eusebio Ochoa hated Ojo del Muerto and yet he was always drawn back to it. The last time he came back to it, he was murdered by Anselo Abeyta, who took a piece of the true *derrotero* from his body. Your father hated the Espantosas and yet he, too, came to Ojo del Muerto in his search for the Lost Killdevil. Someone killed him there, and the blame fell on Marcos Padilla, who died in his turn because he had another piece of the true *derrotero*. So Buck Coulter ended up with that piece of the *derrotero* as well as the one Anselmo Abeyta had taken from Eusebio Ochoa.

"I first became suspicious of something out on the Lagarto Desierto when I noticed a peculiar marking on the *derrotero,* but it had been almost obliterated, and I couldn't be sure. I thought it might possibly be the numeral eight, with about half of the right side missing. So!" He took a charred stick and traced a crude numeral 3 on the rock wall behind the fire. "But if it had been the *other* half of the numeral eight, as I thought it was, it would have looked like this." He traced a reversed numeral 3 on the wall, or Σ. "If I had realized then that it was a reversed three, I would have known that it symbolized *reversing the meaning of all other signs we had found*. So the *derrotero* was authentic enough, but we were following it in the wrong direction, *away* from Ojo del Muerto. I think your grandfather knew about it but was perhaps waiting until the rest of us were gone before he actually hunted for it. I think that perhaps he had found the reversing symbol and had destroyed it."

She nodded. "It would be like him," she said. "So all the time men were using Ojo del Muerto as a starting place in their hunt for the Lost Killdevil, it was actually the end of the search. But you don't know for certain *exactly* where it is, Wes."

He grinned at her. "When I dived into that third pool, fully expecting to break my fool neck, my hands touched something deep beneath the water. At first I thought it might be a submerged pipe, but it wasn't. It was log cribbing, Lucy. Beneath the water of that third pool is the mouth of an ancient mine shaft that is cribbed with logs."

"But you still don't know for sure!"

Wes leaned back against the wall and looked into the flickering embers of the fire. "I remembered something as I broke water. Before the Civil War there had been only two pools at Ojo del Muerto. Everyone seemed to think that the third pool had been formed simply by the overflow from the other two pools, but it was far deeper than either of the first two pools. I figured if it had been formed from overflow, it couldn't be as deep as it was or it would have been a seep pool just like the others. Whoever had worked that mine in ancient times had taken what they wanted from it and had left, perhaps driven off by the Apaches, which is most likely. I think they might have plugged the mouth of the shaft with earth and then cut an underground channel from the second pool and flooded over the mine entrance. Jesus Melgosa knew that."

"But, then, you can't get into the mine without

pumping it out," she said. "I know enough about such mines from what Granddad told me to know it would be almost, if not actually, impossible to keep up with the flow of water. I think they meant to hide it forever."

Wes shook his head. "If they were shrewd enough to hide it as they did, they were shrewd enough to figure out another way to get their *oro* if they ever came back again. Somewhere near Ojo del Muerto there could possibly be another way into that mine, somewhere above the water level. I think that's where Jesus Melgosa got his *oro,* and no one else has ever been able to find it."

"What about Buck Coulter?" she said. "He *knows* it is there, Wes."

Wes shook his head. "He knows he has twenty-four hours to make it to the border. He knows I intend to turn him in at that time. Buck values his neck more than he does the Lost Killdevil. Even if he found the hidden entrance, he could hardly take the time to get any *oro* out of it. The telegraph lines will be humming about him in twenty-four hours, and perhaps one of the biggest manhunts in the history of the Territory of Arizona will begin. No, Lucy, Buck Coulter will never get any good out of the Lost Killdevil."

She searched his lean, thoughtful face. "And you? What about you, Wes?"

He drew her close and kissed her. "Right now I've had more than my fill of these bloody mountains."

The rain drummed down, and the fire died out, but neither of them paid any attention to it.

EIGHTEEN

A fine mizzle was drifting down onto the muddy streets of Eden City. The San Augustin was running bank-full, and its dull roaring could be heard throughout the town. Wes Yardigan stood at the window of his room in the Miner's Rest, looking down onto the wide expanse of Front Street, rutted and muddy, with the yellow lamplight reflecting from the many puddles and pools that dotted the street. Somewhere out in the wet and windy darkness Buck Coulter was likely nearing the border. Wes looked across the street to the pillared, four-square clock that stood on the corner of Front and Prescott in front of the Ranchers and Miners Trust Company. It was five minutes to eleven. The telegraph office closed at twelve on Saturday nights. Wes had already given Buck more than the twenty-four hours he had granted him. The trails would be thick with mud, and the usually dry streambeds would be bank-full like the San Augustin.

Somehow the room seemed to close in on him. Voices seemed to thread through his mind, as though he were suffering delusions. It was the room he had shared with Curly Killigrew and Anselmo Abeyta. "You got any hard feelings toward me?" Curly had asked before he had ridden to his death. "I didn't want to leave without clearing that up, Wes."

Wes slowly shaped a cigarette. "It is said that one must always come back to the Espantosas, is that not so?" Anselmo Abeyta had asked Wes that question as they were riding to Eden City. "What is up there, Señor Wes? Much gold? Perhaps the wealth of a Montezuma?" There had been more understanding sympathy in the Mexican's soft voice than there had been ridicule.

Wes lighted the cigarette. "Go on," Luke Fairbairn had said. "Go on with your three friends, Yardigan. Maybe you'll find the Lost Killdevil and maybe you'll find something else. Something you may not expect to find." The old man had been a better prophet than Wes had realized.

Wes tied his tie and swung his gunbelt around his waist, buckling it and settling it. He withdrew the Colt and checked it. He shrugged into his coat and looked at himself in the mirror. His face was faintly wreathed with cigarette smoke and somehow it seemed older to Wes. The Espantosas have a way of quickly aging a man. He put on his hat and slicker and turned out the lamp. He had plenty of time before the telegraph office closed, but he could not stay in that room any longer.

Wes stopped at the corner of Front and Prescott and

looked up at the rain-streaked windows of the President Grant suite in the Territorial House. They were bright with lamplight. A warmth and comfort seemed to emanate from the suite. Buck Coulter was riding for his life at that very minute, with his once-shattered leg stiffening in the rain and the cold of the night. Wes crossed Prescott Street and looked down toward Sophie Belaire's establishment. The brightly lighted lower-floor windows shone through the rain, while the upper windows had either a very subdued light within them or were completely dark. Business as usual, he thought as he stepped up on the muddy boardwalk.

He looked back over his shoulder at the clock. It was quarter past eleven. The office was in the next block. He angled across Front Street through the hock-deep mud and stepped up in front of the Buckhorn. The place was roaring. Wes looked down the street to the dim lights of the telegraph office. "There's still time for a drink," he said aloud.

Wes opened the door of the Buckhorn, walked in, and stopped at the end of the long bar. The garish lights and sparkling fixtures hurt his eyes. "Rye," he said to the bartender. The man watched Wes out of the corner of his eye as he placed glass and bottle in front of Wes. As Wes poured the drink the bartender walked to the far end of the bar and said something to a waiter. As Wes sipped half his drink he looked up into the dark, heavy-lidded eyes of Duke Draegar.

"Where's Coulter?" said Duke.

Wes lowered the glass. "Quién sabe?" he said.

"I asked you a question," said Duke.

"So you did," said Wes politely, "and I answered it."

"Not the way I wanted it, Yardigan."

"We can't have everything," said Wes philosophically.

Duke's eyes shifted a little. "Is he up in those mountains?"

"Not that I know of."

The eyes flicked down and then up again as Duke appraised Wes. "Where are Killigrew and Abeyta?"

"Quién sabe?" murmured Wes. He was sorry now that

167

he had walked into the Buckhorn. Sorry that the price of one drink would go into Duke's pocket.

"You went after the Killdevil," said Duke.

Eyes flicked toward the two men. It was common knowledge that Buck Coulter and three companions had gone after Killdevil and that the Galeras Bunch had been seen heading that way, and some had said that old Luke Fairbairn had gone back up there again. Odd that none of them had been seen again except that saddle drifter by the name of Yardigan.

Duke slowly rubbed a fat jowl. "Coulter owes me plenty," he said.

"That so?" said Wes.

"You knew about it!"

Wes nodded. "It's Buck's business, not mine."

The eyes flicked down and up again. "You were partners, eh, Yardigan? Where are the others?" Draegar looked around. "Isn't it kind of odd that Yardigan walks unmarked out of the Espantosas, all *alone*?"

"He brought that Fairbairn girl back with him," said a bearded man.

"Maybe he brought something else with him, too," said Duke. "The only reason Buck Coulter sent for him out on the Lagarto was because Yardigan here is the only living man who could have possibly found the Lost Killdevil."

Wes emptied his glass and clenched it in a big hand. "Seems to me, Draegar," he said softly, "you're a helluva lot more interested in whether or not I found Killdevil than you are in what happened to Buck Coulter and the others." He looked up at Duke. "Even if I had found the Killdevil, you cold-gutted shark, and Buck Coulter died in the finding of it, you wouldn't get a centavo out of the deal."

"I've got rights," said Duke.

Wes laughed. "Draegar, sometimes I find you hard to believe."

"I'm real enough to take your measure," blustered Duke.

The door swung open, and Brogan the liveryman came in looking quickly from side to side as though searching for someone. "Wes!" he said. "I just saw Buck Coulter up the street! He's looking for ye!"

It suddenly grew very quiet in the Buckhorn. A waiter dropped a glass at the back of the room, and a roulette wheel whirred slowly to a stop. Feet shifted on the floor, and a man softly set his glass down on the bar.

Brogan came up beside Wes. "He's got that look on his face, Wes. What the hell happened between him and ye up in thim damned mountains?"

The damned fool, thought Wes. He could have made it over the border by now.

"Maybe we can get this thing settled now," said Duke.

Wes looked up at him. "What makes you think *you* ever had any importance in this thing, Draegar?" Wes looked at Brogan. "Where is he?"

"A block up. He was standing in the shadows of the old burned-out Traveler's Hotel."

Wes nodded. The two-story building was a burned-out shell at the eastern end of the block, and across the side street was the telegraph office. "The telegraph office still open?" asked Wes.

Brogan nodded. "The night man is still on. Why?"

Wes shook his head. He reached for the rye bottle, closed a hand on it, and then shoved it back. No man could face Buck Coulter with the least impairment of his skill. There were two people in Eden City that night who could testify against Buck Coulter, a man who had killed three times in his lust for gold and who would kill again if anyone stood in his way. Wes was quite positive that Buck Coulter had come back to Eden City to shut the only two mouths that could incriminate him or to use the Coulter 'charm' on Wes Yardigan. This was something Wes had not anticipated. He looked about that crowded but quiet barroom. There was no use in shooting off his mouth. Who would believe him? Buck Coulter was still a hero, a living legend to many men in that room.

"Come on, Brogan," said Wes. He walked toward the door.

"You didn't pay for the drink, Yardigan!" the bartender called out.

Wes turned a little. "You can take it out of my estate," he said.

"What are you going to do, Yardigan?" said Duke Draegar.

"Come and see," said Wes. "If you've got the guts to do it."

Wes closed the door behind him and gripped Brogan by the arm. "Is Lucy at the house?"

"Yes," said the liveryman.

"Go get her out of there! Tell her I said so. Tell her Coulter is back in town with blood in his eye. I've got to get a wire off to the sheriff. There's no one in this town who'd help me take Coulter."

"For God's sake, Wes! What do ye want to take *him* for?" said the Irishman in astonishment.

"If anything happens to me, you get Lucy out of town this very night. Either get her to the sheriff or keep her hidden until you can reach the sheriff."

"I can't believe it," said Brogan. "What is it the man has done?"

Wes looked down the dim, rain-misted street. "If I stop him, you'll know soon enough. If he stops me, it won't matter unless you get Lucy to the sheriff. I haven't got the time to talk about it now." He looked over his shoulder at the clock in front of the Ranchers and Miners Trust. It was twenty-five minutes to twelve. "Go on, man!" he snapped at Brogan.

Wes peeled off his slicker. He ran through the narrow area between the Buckhorn and the next building and cast his slicker over a fence when he reached the yard. He skirted a row of privies and slipped through a partially opened gateway into the alley. It was thick with churned mud, and the redolence of manure came up about him as his boots dug into it. He reached the western side of the burned-out Travelers Hotel and stopped. He peered around the corner, looking up toward Front Street. The bottom floor of the building was a jungle of burned-out lumber, piles of plaster, rusted piping, and other hardware. At regular intervals rose the iron stanchions that had held up the second floor, which was now gapped with great holes into which hung burned flooring. Water

dripped and pattered down through the building and puddled in the low places.

Wes slipped into the building and stopped behind a
stanchion, scanning the front area of the building. He
could see the dim yellow lights of the telegraph office on
the corner of Front and Carleton. As he looked back
again he caught a faint movement at the front of the
building. Buck Coulter never missed a trick. He had
posted himself in the most strategic spot for whatever it
was he had in his mind. He could see Front Street both
sides of the street, east and west. Likely he had seen Wes
go into the Buckhorn. He had the telegraph office under
surveillance and he could look through the open ground
floor of the Travelers Hotel clear through to the alleyway.
No man could get to that telegraph office unseen by
Buck.

What in God's name did he want? Why had he come
back to Eden City? Supposing Wes had already sent the
telegram at the expiration of the time limit he had given
Buck? Buck would have walked into a trap. Then slow
realization came to Wes. Buck had gambled on Wes'
feeling toward him. *He had gambled on the fact that Wes
had not or would not send the telegram.*

Wes eased his way into the dangerous building. The
flooring had great gaps in it overhung by the burned and
shattered wood like mats of coarse growths. Wes worked
his way over to the wall and kept close to it. He wasn't
even sure why he was doing it at all. He saw the movement again up at the front of the building and was sure he
recognized the tall, lean figure of Buck Coulter.

Wes dropped his hand to the butt of his Colt. He
narrowed his eyes. He had no way of knowing what Buck
had in mind; of how he felt; of why he had really come
back from the Espantosas. Wes slipped from one wall
stanchion to the other with the rain pattering down from
the great holes in the roof and running down from the
upper floor. The place stank of wet plaster and charred
wood and of human waste left by passersby.

Wes was twenty feet away from Buck when the man
turned and looked directly toward him, although Wes was
almost sure he had not been seen. "Who's there?" said

Buck. His arms hung by his sides. Maybe he had no intention of drawing, but he did not wear a slicker. That was enough for Wes Yardigan. "It's you, isn't it, Wes?" added Buck.

The man was a devil! No wonder he had been able to out-Apache even the Apaches themselves.

"Wes?" said Buck.

"It's me, Buck," said Wes and he moved to one side even as he spoke.

"What are you hiding in there for, boy? You're liable to fall into a hole and break your neck."

"I don't want to stop a slug," said Wes.

"You haven't sent that telegram?"

There was no use in lying. Buck knew damned well that Wes had not sent it. "No," said Wes.

"But you still intend to, eh?"

"That's the size of it, Buck," said Wes. He shifted again.

Rain pattered and dripped throughout the building. It was very quiet for a Saturday night on Front Street, but likely by now the word had passed from bar to bar that Wes Yardigan was out in the dark and wet looking for Buck Coulter, or maybe it was the other way around. Either way, mister, it would add up to something big, something the likes of which Eden City had never seen and might never see again.

"You haven't lost anything," said Buck.

"Three men are dead up in the Espantosas."

"What does that have to do with you? It was all part of the game, Wes."

"Murder?"

"Murder, hell!" said Buck. "It was merely elimination, boy."

"And I'm next," said Wes.

"How you talk, boy," said Buck. "Look, Wes, you can do anything you like. Go back to the Lagarto. Buy that ranch. Stay here and get a job. If I can get back as Chief Marshal, you'll be my right-hand man. How's that, Wes?"

Wes moved again, fading into the deepest shadow he could find and crouching a little to keep a big pile of trash and junk between him and Buck. "It's all over," said Wes.

"Up the spout. Get the hell out of town. Keep moving. You might make it."

Buck shook his head. "Too far, and I'm too tired to run and keep on running, Wes."

Wes dropped his hand to his Colt and eased sideways. He was expecting a shot, but it came so swiftly that it surprised him. The slug slammed into one of the iron stanchions and keened eerily from it while the thunder of the gun report slammed and echoed throughout the burned-out hulk of the hotel. Wes threw himself sideways as he drew, thrusting forward his Colt and triggering off a round to keep Buck from shooting at once. Wes fell over a pipe as Buck fired again. The slug seemed to whisper past Wes' ear. Boots thudded on the dangerous weakened flooring, and Wes fired at the sound. He heard Buck laugh. The sonofabitch was invulnerable.

Buck did not move again. Wes bellied along the floor, feeling the wet work through his shirt and undershirt. He lay flat at the lip of a gaping hole with his head around the base of a stanchion. He could see the dim lights of the telegraph office across the street and he knew well enough it didn't matter now. Now it was a question of *who* died this rainy night in the Travelers Hotel.

Something clicked against a stanchion behind Wes. He turned his head and raised it. A shot struck the floor inches from his face, spraying it with mud and wet plaster. He wiped it away even as he rolled over behind a pile of rusted piping. Buck had suckered him into that one by tossing something behind Wes.

It was quiet again. Wes' eyes flicked back and forth, but there was no sight of Buck and there would be no sound from that cat-footed man, limp and all. Wes eased up behind a stanchion and thumbed the muck from his eye-sockets. The rain beat down harder for a moment and then diminished to a drizzle again. Wes stepped slowly backward against the west wall. Something struck hard against the wall at his left side. Wes did the border shift from right to left hand as he felt the restraint of something holding his left upper sleeve to the wall behind him. He placed his hand on the haft of a knife, and his blood seemed to congeal. He had seen that damned knife in

173

action too many times not to know what it could do to a man's throat. He freed it from the wooden paneling of the wall and tossed it behind a pile of trash as he went down on his knees and worked his way toward the front of the building. He could feel a wet trace of blood running down his left arm where the tip of the knife had sliced the flesh. Fear began to ride his broad back. The man could see like a cat!

Buck's six-gun flamed in the darkness at the eastern side of the building, and the slug slammed into the west wall inches from Wes. Wes fired twice at the flash. One of the slugs smashed the window of the telegraph office across the street, and the light went out.

"Close, boy, close!" Buck called out, and the sound of the voice came many feet away from where Wes had aimed his shots and much closer to Wes.

Wes wiped the rain and sweat from his face. The butt of his Colt was greasy with sweat, and he could feel the cold sweat sliding down his body. I'm going to die, he thought. He's going to kill me and he can do it when he feels like it.

He saw the movement at the front of the building and he ran toward the street. A bullet smashed into a stanchion as he saw Buck leap sideways out into the muck of the street. Wes ran toward him and saw that deadly Colt come up, and a fraction of a second before Buck fired, Wes himself fired. Something plucked at the top of Wes' hat, and he went belly-flat in the mud and fired up at Buck with his last round.

Powdersmoke wreathed around Buck as he staggered back with the impact of the soft .44/40 slug. He dropped his fine Colt into the muck of the street and then went down on one knee. For a few seconds he looked at Wes and then he held out his right hand, almost as though in farewell. The hand closed spasmodically into a fist, and Buck Coulter fell face forward into the muck and filth of the street.

"My God!" a man yelled from a doorway. "Wes Yardigan has killed Buck Coulter!"

Wes got up and sheathed his empty six-gun. He walked toward Buck and rolled him over onto his back. The gray

174

eyes opened, but they were no longer clear. Buck coughed. A thread of bright blood leaked out of the side of his mouth. "It was better this way," he said huskily. "It's all I had to leave to you, boy. If you use it, use it well. So long, Wes." His head sagged back, and he was gone forever.

Boots thudded in the muck. Doors slammed open and windows slammed up. Men were yelling and calling out the incredible news to each other. Wes stood up. The four-square clock struck the hour of twelve. Eden City had had its usual man for dinner that Saturday night, but it would never have another one like Buck Coulter served up to it.

"I always said Wes Yardigan was the fastest of the two of them," said a loudmouth from the sidewalk.

"Not in Coulter's prime, he wasn't!" said another.

"There's always some gun faster'n you, someplace, sometime," opined another authority.

"Yardigan couldn't hold a patch onto Coulter!"

"Who's got the slug in his guts?" challenged another. "Ain't *that* the final sayso?"

Wes picked up Buck's expensive, rain-soaked Stetson and placed it over the pale, mud-stained face. In New Mexico they had once nicknamed Buck Coulter 'Death in a Stetson hat.' Wes tilted his head to one side and slowly drew a coat sleeve across his face. His eyes were unseeing. Those who had been crowding forward now stepped hastily aside as he slowly walked toward the marshal's office.

"Hey, Yardigan!" yelled a drunk. "You've inherited everything from your dead friend here. His job, his reputation, and likely Sophie Belaire. Think you can live up to all three of them, Wes Yardigan?"

Brogan was walking Lucy toward Wes. Dick Ledbetter, assistant marshal under Buck Coulter and likely now to succeed him, was with them. Ledbetter looked out into the street where the milling crowd stood about the dead man. "That drunk is right, Wes," he said quietly. He studied Wes. "The man who killed Buck Coulter."

Wes looked away. "Do you want me tonight?" he said.

Ledbetter shook his head. "You won't be going anywhere. Tomorrow will be fine. It looked as though he had

175

come after you, Wes. Self-defense, eh?"

Wes nodded. He took Lucy by the arm and walked west on Front Street away from the crowd and against the foot traffic that was hurrying to see the body of Buck Coulter.

Wes turned down Lowell Street toward Bartlett. No one, not even Lucy, would ever know that Buck Coulter could have killed Wes several times in the Travelers Hotel. Even at the last Wes had known that Buck could have killed him. Buck Coulter had not run for the border. He had come back to the only life he really wanted, playing the odds that Wes Yardigan would not turn him in and that someday they could go back for the Lost Killdevil. But there had been an alternative. Buck had planned his own execution at the hand of the man who had been his best friend, a man he might easily have killed instead if he had wanted to do so. Wes passed a hand across his eyes. What was it? His mind refused to think. Had it been suicide? Had it been poetic justice? Lucy might know in time, but she'd never learn it from Wes. Wes would never tell another living soul. At that, he might never be able to figure it out himself.

Bartlett Street was empty. The lodestone of the dead Buck Coulter was drawing everyone to Front Street. She turned to him on the porch of the little cottage. "Will you ever go back for the Lost Killdevil?" she said.

He bent and kissed her. "Someday perhaps. Perhaps not for a long, long time. Perhaps never. I just might, however, if you will give me six strong sons to guard their old man's back while he digs out the gold."

"And the wife?" she asked. "Won't she need six pretty daughters to wait with her at home in the Chiricahua Hills?"

He kissed her again. "We'll hold the thought," he said quietly. They closed the door behind them on Eden City, Buck Coulter, and the Lost Killdevil.